Mary Ann's Mountain

Mary Ann Rose Hart

Savannah, Lawson, Tanya and Curt,

Hope you enjoy the life lessons imparted by your grandfather, Grandmother Kohr, your great-great grandparents, and great-uncles.

Merry Christmas!

Aunt Mary Ann

Illustration by Tom Heggie.

Photographs by Photo Innovations.

First published by Dog Ear Publishing
4010 W. 86th Street, Ste H
Indianapolis, IN 46268
www.dogearpublishing.net

ISBN: 978-1-4575-3266-5

Library of Congress Control Number: has been applied for

This book is printed on acid-free paper.

Printed in the United States of America

This book is dedicated to my ninety-four-year-old mother, my most precious grandparents who lived to be 100 and 102, to my three brothers and my cousins who shared the journey, and to a special aunt and uncle. To my grandnieces and grand-nephews, I hope you enjoy seeing your name in print. I, also, hope you come to have an appreciation for our family's heritage. I thank my former fifth-grade students for inspiring and encouraging me to write. The wonderful teachers at Clintwood High School, which sits deep in the mountainous coalfields of Virginia, will never be forgotten. David, thanks for your encouragement and support!

Contents

My Mountain Home

Some outsiders call us folks who live in the mountainous coalfields of Virginia hillbillies or rednecks. Mother says we are neither. Mother says that we are just hardworking mountain people with the same hopes and dreams as everyone else.

Our farm sits on a high ridge overlooking the Cumberland Mountains to the west and the Clinch Mountains to the east. Our mountain is so high that at night, I can almost touch the moon and the stars. Our particular ridge is called Caney Ridge, named for the courageous Kane family, settlers in this part of the state. For some reason, the first letter of the spelling of our ridge was spelled with "C" instead of "K". I guess spellings change same as our mountain changes from season to season.

In the 1700s, our country was still ruled by the king of England, who forbade the colonists to settle in the Appalachian Mountains. There just weren't enough British soldiers to protect the newcomers from the sometimes unfriendly natives. But after making the treacherous journey across the Atlantic Ocean to eventually set down roots in the Appalachian Mountains of Virginia, Mother says, those independently minded Scotch-Irish weren't going to let a king from across the Atlantic Ocean tell them what to do! Family after family continued to settle our mountains. My very own family used rubies, knives, farm tools, pots and pans, and even one fancy rifle to barter for land the Cherokee Nation had inhabited for thousands of years. The Cherokees soon realized that trinkets and tools were not a fair trade for their land. In retaliation, they murdered interlopers like John Douglas and took children captive. I'm part Cherokee. I guess that eventually, the Cherokee and the Scotch-Irish figured out how to get along.

There is never a dull moment on our mountain. Even with doing the same chores every day, it never gets boring. Mommy Laurie, my grandmother, usually does the milking, but my grandfather, Poppy, is milking this morning because he is waiting on the lumber shipment for the home he is building over on Longs Fork. While Poppy is milking, I muck out Ole Cherry's stall; then, I fill the stall's manger with fresh hay for the milk cow's feeding tonight.

Poppy breaks the silence. "Your grandmother is shore goin' to be pleased with Ole Cherry today. A gallon and a half of milk! It looks like Ole Cherry ate well yesterday. There's enough cream here for your grandmother to add to the rest that she skimmed off the milk this week to make butter. Little Chank, looks like you and the churn are goin' to be friends today."

"Can't wait, Poppy! There's nothing better than oatmeal drowned in a good dollop of fresh butter. But I'd have to say that Mommy's pinto beans with cornbread or her Sunday fried chicken with tomato gravy can't be beat! Guess you'd be lost without butter to slather on your molassie biscuit, wouldn't ya?"

Poppy agrees wholeheartedly.

Fall brings cool weather, and that means hog-killing time. I tell Poppy, "Everyone around us is butcherin' their hogs this week. The boys at school think it's a vacation to get off school to help. They are just daft in the head! Poppy, I wish Sadie Mae could stay a piglet."

"Now, don't you go namin' those piglets. You know they have to be sold when full grown," Poppy reminds me for the hundredth time.

We have only piglets left right now because we just sold our hogs to the butcher. Piglets are fun to watch. You see, they have this game where all ten piglets pile on top of each other like they are trying to build a haystack, only the haystack gets real slippery from the mud in which they wallow. As one piglet tumbles down from the top of the heap, another piglet climbs up. The game ends when they all tumble right back into the mud. It's a riot!

My brothers, cousins, and I aren't allowed to name or pet the farm animals that will be sold or used for our own food. I didn't mean to let it slip that I broke Poppy's rule.

But no matter what folks say, piglets aren't all alike. You see, Sadie Mae has a big brown circle around her one squinty blue eye. She trots those little stubby legs over to greet me. As I pick up a bucket of water to pour over her, she squeals in delight. Sadie Mae would like for me to scratch behind her ears all day long. I would, if she took a bath more often.

Watching me as I pour water over Sadie Mae, Poppy says, "You know there's a lot to be learnt from those piglets? They're a lot like people. Each piglet is full of the same hopes and dreams that it will reach the summit. There's a lot to be said about never givin' up. After your daddy died, your mother didn't give up. She returned to school to finish her education. Your mother is turnin' her own hopes and dreams into a reality. But don't you go namin' those piglets, you hear?"

Soon, Mother and my three brothers will come home to live on the farm for good. For the last three years, they have lived in Emory, Virginia, where Mother is getting her teaching degree at a school called Emory and Henry College. Mother said she needed a way to make a living after my daddy died and that she had always wanted to teach, so she took the boys with her and set out to fulfill her dream. They will come back to our mountain for good after Christmas. Mother will drive herself and the boys to the high school in town in her new 1957 Chevrolet. There, she will teach Latin, English, and social studies.

I live on the farm with my grandparents. I don't mind. Mother explained to me that I have to live with my grandparents because she can't afford a sitter to take care of me after school. My two older brothers play football on the high school team. Although Thurston, the brother closest to me in age, is too young to play football, the coach gave him the job as team manager. That way, all my brothers can go home after practice at the same time, start supper, and begin their homework.

Mother says that football gives my brothers an outlet for excess energy, as well as supervision. My brothers say that football is not just a game for them. They are hoping for scholarships to college.

I was a little baby when my daddy died. I never knew him. Daddy was a coal miner and a hog farmer before being called up by the Navy to fight the Japanese in World War II. After coming home from an island called Guam, my daddy spent a lot of time at a veterans hospital a long way from our mountain. My brothers remember the sad day when Mother got a telegram saying Daddy had lost his last battle.

My two older brothers tell about adventures with Daddy. Sometimes, my aunts and uncles tell stories about Daddy's love for his family. I believe Daddy was special to a lot of people. From what I'm told, he could find a funny side to just about anything. Sometimes, I meet up with folks I don't even know, who tell me about Daddy. One stranger said to me one day at Miss Winnie's store, "You're Beuford's little girl, ain't-cha? Well, let me tell ya, when we were no bigger'n a mite, me and him used to go coon huntin' together. We shore had us a good time. There was this time when..." The stranger went on and on.

Another time at an all-county chorus practice, this older girl ran over to me, hugged me, and exclaimed, "Your daddy was a saint! One time when my daddy was injured in the coal mine down at Clincho, your father brought us groceries every week right up to the time that my daddy was able to go back to work. Our family of seven would have starved if it hadn't been for your dad."

The stories are many, and I will always keep them in my heart. Wish I could have known my dad!

Yes, life on our mountain is full of happy times, sad times, and more entertainment than there could ever be at the town cinema.

I am lucky to have my grandfather. Most every night while Mommy is cooking supper, Poppy likes to help me with my math homework. Our goal is to solve a single word problem two or three different ways before we quit. If I don't have word problems for homework, we make up some that are fun and challenging all at the same time!

Poppy must be pretty smart, because as a ten-year-old, he did his lessons with the sixth graders in the same two-room school I now attend. One night he confided in me, "When Paw left Maw, I had to quit school to help on the farm. My education was sacrificed for choppin' down trees and cuttin' 'em up for firewood, or else we would have frozen. For a ten-year-old, that was mighty hard work! All my life, I've regretted not gittin' an education. When your mother and her sister and brothers come along, I did what I could to see to it that they got their schoolin'. I regret I couldn't give 'em all a proper education. Your own mother proves that learnin' is something you never grow too old for! Yes, siree, I'm proud of her determination to get a college degree."

Poppy farms, raises beef cattle with my uncles, and builds houses. Poppy is the local beekeeper, too. In these mountains, just about everybody has to work at more than one job to make ends meet. Most of the men around here are coal miners. Coal-mining days ended for my grandfather when he helped rescue miners trapped inside a collapsed mine. On that day, Poppy prayed, "Lord, if you let me git out of this mine safe and sound, I'll never step foot in another mine again!" He never did.

This morning when we get back to the house with the milk, there is a man waiting with his family in the living room. Poppy doesn't show his surprise at having company this early on a Saturday morning. Folks often come to our house just to catch the breeze on the front porch when the weather allows. In cooler weather, visitors warm themselves in front of the stone fireplace and talk farming, religion, politics, and the happenings up and down Caney Ridge.

Standing to shake hands with Poppy, the man explains, "Monroe, I am second cousin to Rupert, who is first cousin to Albert, who is a friend of your uncle Charlie. My name is Orby, and this here is my wife, Bertie. These are my young'uns. I own some coal mines down near Jenkins, Kentucky. We like it down there, and we want you to build us a home." The man begins to unroll his house plans.

Poppy interrupts the man and talks to him like he has known him all his life. "Orby, you know, I can't promise to get around to you for a year or more. I've just started a big ranch house down at Longs Fork. There's a lot of brick and stonework to do. I have a second chicken house to build for my grandson, and I have to add on to that little house up there on the hill for my daughter and her four children. They'll be movin' back to our mountain before long."

"Well, Monroe, we'll wait as long as needed in order to git the best carpenter and bricklayer around. And I understand that you don't overcharge. We can negotiate the wages to suit us both, I'm sure!"

Mommy calls me to the kitchen to start the churning while Poppy discusses house plans with our visitors. Guess Poppy has his next job.

"It seems folk shore seek out this mountain," mutters Mommy. "That couple must really want Monroe to build 'em a house. Why else would anyone come up the mountain at this time of day, and with snow clouds a-loomin' in the sky, at that? It seems to me that a simple phone call would have done the job."

"Mommy, I think folks just like to talk to Poppy one-on-one. They just want to see if Poppy is who folks say he is. Maybe they want to see the beauty of our mountain as well!"

"Poppy needs to charge more for his labor. He wants to do right by folk, I suppose, but people take advantage of that! And I don't like it one bit when he has to be away from home for weeks at a time. We already paid our dues on that score, what with him livin' in those ramshackle bunk houses when he cut timber for the Mountain Laurel Timber Company! More than oncet, he woke up with snow a-coverin' 'im because of cracks in the shoddy wood sidin'. If I had my druthers, I'd have 'im turn down the job."

Even though she is upset, Mommy wants to do things right, too. She never lets anyone leave our home without a little something to fill their bellies. Like others, this family will trek down the mountain with a poke full of ham biscuits, freshly made fried apple pies, and a quart of cold milk to hold them until they get home, which is hours away. Mommy knows that in our mountains, you could find yourself in a pickle if you need gasoline, a meal, or a place to sleep. However, the woods along the side of the road can serve pretty handily as a potty. I know that for a fact! Mommy carries toilet paper on our visits to her sisters down in Kentucky. At least our visitors will have some good snacks going over, around, and through the mountains.

Poppy has many talents besides building a good house. When he sings, Poppy's soft voice sounds like a lullaby. Just hearing Poppy sing in church fills me with peace. At one time, he played the banjo but doesn't have time for such nowadays. A real good picker in his younger days, Poppy played with Mother Maybelle when her family came home to visit the Carter clan up the road. Maybelle and the Carter family are famous around these parts. Poppy never did play with Ralph and Carter Stanley, though. The Stanley Brothers were Daddy's boyhood friends, growing up on an adjoining farm just a stone's throw over the next ridge. Playing gospel and bluegrass with Bill Monroe and the Clinch Mountain Boys, Daddy's friends got their names known everywhere. These mountains sure do have a lot of good singers, pickers, and fiddlers. I wish Poppy would sing and play more; then, the mountains would really sing!

Mother believes that mountain music is one thing that grounds our mountain folks. According to her, the love of the fiddle and singing is as much a part of our heritage as is the right to vote in free elections. Mother says that we should take care to preserve our heritage.

The fiddle can sure make the toes tap a jig. I'm learning how to square dance in school. Clogging doesn't seem too ladylike to me or to some of my friends, so it's mostly boys who participate in competitions to see who can last the longest and add the most new steps.

Although I have never seen my grandfather dance a jig, I have heard him laugh. I love to hear Poppy laugh. I wrote this poem to give him for his birthday.

Poppy's Laugh

Poppy has an unusual laugh—
"Hee, hee, hee" comes up from his diaphragm.
So tickled one gets, one just has to join in.

Ethnic jokes are not his choice,
But just plain old funnies of unwary men
Whose very own ignorance gets the best of them.

Yes, Poppy can laugh from time to time.
His laughter engages many a friend.
Wish I could bottle it to hear again and again and again!

Poppy can be funny. With a twinkle in those pale blue eyes, he chuckles when he says, "My ears are so-o-o big, they could sail me from here to China!" (His gigantic ears are fodder for family jokes!) I guess Poppy learned a lot about the Chinese who came in to work on the railroads that haul coal and timber out of our mountains. My nickname is Little Chank. "Chank" in Chinese means a small, round piece of marble. I'm small, all right—short and skinny! Poppy is always saying that I need more meat on my bones!

After the rails were laid, some Chinese and Hungarians stayed in this part of the world. They worked alongside Poppy at the coke ovens down at Tom's Creek. Poppy can tell us funnies from time to time, but he never makes fun of anyone because of their looks, their way of talking, or their way of life. Mother says that we mountain folks have borne the sting of too many jokes. My family believes that we should treat all people with respect.

Another poem I wrote for a school contest explains how Poppy came to have this farm. During the Great Depression of 1929, it seems every family in these parts was hungry and broke. The story goes like this: Great-Grandpa Clay, Poppy's daddy, just up and left the family. Mommy Laurie says Grandpa Clay did not abide by his responsibilities to his family, so it was left for Poppy and his mother, my great-grandma Nancy, to pay off the farm. This poem tells how they managed that feat.

Onions of Gold

Did you know that 'tater onions are gold?
Yep! Believe it or not . . .
Poppy told me so!

Poppy's paw was not always around,
so Poppy, the youngest, and his mother
were left to save the farm one way or another.

Onions it was that paid the debts—
little, gnarly clumps of gold
grown in ground that Poppy hoed.

So strong the flavor, so strong the smell!
But times were hard and money was scarce
and the will to succeed made Great-Grandma fierce.

For on her horse to town she would go
to sell those onions, proclaiming the good
found in each juicy bite of this mighty food.

Tears of joy those onions brought
to Poppy and his faithful mother,
proving that from hardship one can recover.

As it turns out, Great-Grandma was right,
for the debt was paid, the farm was theirs,
a prize to be cherished by all the heirs!

Did you know that 'tater onions are gold?
Yep! Believe it or not . . .
Poppy told me so!

Poppy must see his own hopes and dreams for our farm and his family in those little piglets as they keep trying to climb to the top of the heap. Mother says that my grandfather and his mother gave their today for our tomorrow. This mountain farm is the prize, and it is our home!

More Than Book Learnin'

"Mary Ann, before you do your chores, I need for you to take some of Poppy's honey up to Winnie's store. You'll need to bring back some staples. I've already called in my list, and the little red wagon is already loaded."

It's a good thing that Mommy put some towels in between the jars of that golden honey to keep them from bumping into each other and breaking. Our dirt road is full of ruts and holes. No matter—the main roads have ruts and holes, too, even though they are paved.

By the time I pull the wagon up the last hill, it's getting heavy. Miss Winnie holds open the big oak double doors, and I pull the wagon right into the store. As Miss Winnie stacks the jars onto the shelves, she tells me to get a free peppermint stick out of one of the three-cent candy jars sitting on the counter. Miss Winnie lets me believe it is her treat for being the delivery girl. I know better. I know that this is Poppy's secret treat for me.

When the wagon is empty, Miss Winnie exchanges staples for the honey. She loads the wagon with cornmeal, flour, sugar, salt, and two Cokes, which are for medicinal purposes only.

Once I faked a stomach ache just to get some sips of Coke. When my friends came to double Dutch, Mommy told them I couldn't jump rope because I was sick. Never again did I lie. Lies have a way to come back and haunt you.

Nothing stays a secret for long on this mountain. I know this because as I leave the store with Cokes in tow, Miss Winnie grins at me saying, "Now, be wise. You must decide if a sip or two of

Coke is an equitable exchange for not gittin' to play hopscotch or jump rope with your friends." Will I never hear the end of it?

It seems I'm learning a lot of lessons these days. Yesterday on the playground, Danny called Ling a "slant-eyed Chink." Miss McCoy, the upper-school teacher, must have gotten wind of it, because she nixed this name-calling during our history lesson about the building of the great transcontinental railroad system that connected our country from the Atlantic to the Pacific.

Miss McCoy lectured, "You know the railroads would not have been built without the backbreaking work of men from countries like Ireland and China. The Chinese immigrants made up most of the labor force for the building of the transcontinental railway. They were paid practically nothing for this monumental task. Hundreds of these Chinese died while drilling blasting holes in the rock, and we know from our own coal miners how dangerous that is! Freezing temperatures and avalanches in the High Sierras killed hundreds more. In our own mountains, the Chinese helped lay the railroad tracks that take timber and coal out to big ports like Norfolk.

"Furthermore, we would not be able to keep all the coal mines or the stone quarries open without the Hungarians and Italians. Our country is still recovering from World War II, and we have a lot of roads, bridges, and new structures to build. We lost a lot of our men in the war. Our country doesn't have the manpower it once had. We need the expertise and the muscle that immigrants bring to our mountains.

"Yes, we should thank the families like Ling's, Angelica's, and Kornel's who came to our country to share their skills with us. It is this diversity of people and the skills they bring with them that make our country strong. We need these newest citizens. Don't forget that! And don't forget that each and every one of us sitting here comes from families who were once immigrants."

Garrison, one of the seventh graders, piped up, "Amen, Miss McCoy. You told 'em good. If that ain't the best lesson I ever heerd, I'll swallow a fly! I'll bet there ain't a teacher in the whole county better'n you!"

Miss McCoy smiled and quietly replied, "Thank you, Garrison. Now, when you have finished those ten algebraic equations, you and I will have a personalized lesson on grammar usage."

Danny countered, "Aw, shucks, Miss McCoy, I know how to talk right! I just forgot for a moment to whom I was speakin', is all."

Snickers circled the room. Ling glanced my way real quick, and I smiled at her. Biting her lip and trying not to cry, she smiled back. Garrison had saved her from being the center of attention. For that, I'm sure, she was grateful.

When I told Poppy about Danny's harsh words, Miss McCoy's response, and Garrison's pronouncement, Poppy smiled with that twinkle in his eyes and said, "Little Chank, I think Garrison knows what he's talkin' about. I do believe you have one good teacher!"

Something else is on my mind tonight. I ask, "Poppy, do you remember my friend Judy? You know, she's the one with hair the color of bright shiny pennies and a crop of freckles across her nose. Her daddy was killed in the coal-mine explosion over at Big Stone Gap last year. Judy is real quiet-like these days. She doesn't talk much, and she hides herself in books so she doesn't have to speak to anyone, not even to me. I don't know what to do. I just know that Judy misses her daddy and a whole lot of words don't make her feel one bit better! What can I do?"

"Not everything has an answer, Little Chank. What Judy needs is a friend. You just be that friend. I'm sorry to say our mountain has a lot of lessons to be learnt that don't come from a book! No, siree, ain't just books that teach us lessons!"

And so, my thoughts are all jumbled as I wonder why bad things happen in our mountains. As my eyes scan the horizon created by what Mother calls those old, wise, and mighty mountains, a peace enters my soul and a quiet comes over me that gives my head time to think about why some people don't accept others as equals and why my friend had to lose her daddy, too. Maybe with time, our mountain will give me answers.

Chicken Poop

Now a fifth grader, I walk with my cousins to the two-room school barely a mile's walk up the road. The lower school has grades one through three. The upper school has grades four through seven. Miss McCoy, the upper-school teacher, lets me take some lessons with the sixth graders.

I love learning about the state of Virginia and the history of the United States. In case you didn't know, Virginians contributed a lot to America's history. Miss McCoy says that while it's good to show pride, we Virginians sometimes forget that Virginia is but a mere state, not our own country. She says that we Virginians often tend to place a little too much stock in the part we played in American history.

At school, the fourth graders have a beautiful new history book about Virginia. I've never seen a book with a shiny cover before. On the cover, the artist painted a picture of a Virginia farm just like ours. The sun bursts over the barn in breathtaking shades of pink, red, orange, and yellow. The Caney Ridge sunrise can explode into splendorous colors, too—colors I never noticed before seeing that new history book. Every morning, just as the sun peeks over the barn and paints the sky, our farm awakens to the sound of animals announcing that it's time to get up and to see what life might bring us all today.

Our farm is a busy place. The barn and the chicken house make for a lot of work. When he comes home to the mountain, Thurston helps take care of the chickens. You see, we sell eggs to the local stores. Because of Thurston's interest in helping to increase the business, Poppy plans to build a second chicken house. Poppy thinks it's admirable that my brother wants to start a college fund with the money he earns.

A chicken house is suffocating, and it stinks! A chicken house has to be shoveled out every few days. I'm here to tell you that five hundred chickens can make some messes! The chickens are free to roam around the chicken house and do as they please wherever they please.

I'm not as fond of the chickens as my grandmother and brother seem to be. When those chickens make big messes in their nesting boxes, the eggs get smeared. Yeah, you get the picture! That's when the boxes have to be emptied and the straw replaced so the eggs stay clean. It's a real pain when the chore has to be done more than once a week!

Virginia Tech helped my grandmother design a chicken house with fans in it. Thankfully, I can now breathe a little better, and the chickens no longer free range in the yard! Shoveling chicken poop became a lot easier with a real chicken house—as long as I wear my galoshes! Too bad there's no such thing as an electric pooper-scooper!

My grandmother keeps records on the kinds of special grains fed the chickens and egg productivity. It must be real important work, because professors drive all the way from Blacksburg to read over Mommy's paperwork and to check out the white leghorns. Students from the agricultural school come to learn about the care and feeding of chickens. I can't imagine why these students look a little green around the gills from their ride up our mountain. Sometimes, before the cars even come to a complete stop, the boys are already throwing open the doors and racing each other to the back of the chicken house. What a pity their weak stomachs keep them from seeing the beauty of our mountains!

Once, I heard a professor ask, "Mrs. Stanley, aren't there any good two-lane roads we can drive back to Blacksburg on?"

Well, now, did he ever step in it!

Mommy retorted, "Well, if the state legislators ever recognize that the good people of Southwest Virginia pay taxes, maybe we would get some good roads. The great state of Virginia refuses to build good roads back here because it's goin' to cost an arm and a leg to dig through these here mountains. Maintainin' these roads is another problem. Coal trucks, snow, and ice all do their damage and add even more to the cost, don't-cha know? Sometimes, I think that we mountain folk are considered to be an ignorant backwoods stepchild and that we just don't know where our taxes are goin'. No, sir, I doubt I'll ever see new roads in these parts in my lifetime."

I never have heard those professors ask my grandmother about roads again. Certain topics can sure stir up her ire. But my grandmother loves her chickens and wants the best for them, so she is eager to listen to the lessons the professors teach their students right there on our mountain. Wanting to keep the help coming, Mommy always offers the professors and students fried apple pies, ham biscuits, and glasses of cold milk straight from the springhouse.

When my friends come to visit, they stand at the chicken house door, holding their noses! No help from them. No getting out of chores when company comes, either. The word has spread around school that I don't get to play much after school. On our farm, we work from the time the sun wakes up until the sun goes to sleep. Pajama parties are out of the question. That's all right by me. I have fun with my friends at school. I love school!

Every afternoon, Mommy and I clean the eggs and sort them by size to place into cartons. Yeah, I want to make sure those nests have clean straw to cut down on poop detail. My brother will be most welcome to this nasty chore. He is so serious about chicken duties that I sometimes think he actually likes those chickens! Guess he still believes the story told him by Aunt Tess when he was only four. Aunt Tess told the poor little thing that he was hatched, not born!

As you can probably tell, for me, those chickens make for the worst farm duty of all! Glad our mountain is big enough to provide us with lots of fresh air!

Pillow Wars and the Mighty Shoe

My grandparents have a dormitory upstairs where my three uncles slept as boys. My brothers sleep there when they come home. Three big wrought-iron beds line up along one wall. Each bed has its own feather tick mattress. A trunk sits at the foot of each bed and holds all the clothes that anyone would ever need. A chifforobe sitting at each end of the dormitory holds suits and such pieces of clothing that need to be on hangers.

In the summers, we take the feather beds outside on every day that promises to be pretty. We lay the beds on sawhorses and beat them with rug beaters until all the dust is gone. During the day, the sun finishes the job. At night, those feather beds smell like pure sunshine and mountain air.

Christmas will be here in a couple of weeks. Yesterday, Mommy and I freshened up the bedrooms because Mother and my brothers are coming home for a weekend break.

I wake up this morning to Mommy and Poppy discussing the upcoming farm business and making plans to buy assorted nuts, oranges, and tangerines for the Christmas stockings.

Poppy says, "I shore hope those boys of Christine's don't give her any more trouble because of the sleepin' quarters upstairs. Sleepin' so close together makes 'em act like a bunch of bantam roosters at times. I'm afraid the last trip home was not very pleasant for Christine."

You see, sometimes, my brothers become real boisterous. The last time they were home, a game of Monopoly turned into an outright war over cheating. Pillow fights are the usual way we solve arguments. When we have pillow fights, which we often do, we have this agreement that we can't laugh too much or make too much noise. That way, we never get caught. The last time, though, the boys' tempers exploded. Pillows started flying. One pillow burst. Yelling erupted.

"You cheated first. You stole one of my houses on Boardwalk!" yelled Dale.

Kyle hollered back, "You snitched a $100 bill from my stack of money!"

The arguing did not stop. Cousins who had been playing Monopoly with us made a hasty exit for home, for they knew my brothers were headed for trouble.

Mother sent up a warning. The warning was not heeded. We did not hear Mother coming up the stairs. When greeted by a cloud of feathers raining everywhere, Mother took off her shoe and proceeded to spank each brother in turn.

My brothers were shocked speechless because they are mostly grown boys. Mostly, grown boys don't get spanked! And with a shoe?

A talking-to is our usual punishment. If Mother feels a talking-to is not sufficient, she puts us all—no matter our ages—in a corner to stand and to think about the error of our ways until we can stand no longer. Another lecture sometimes follows about our responsibilities and proper decorum. Afterwards, Mommy and Poppy remind us that Mother doesn't need the added burden of having to referee fights and arguments. Then, we all feel guilty because we've let Mother down. The guilt weighs heavy upon our hearts, and we don't misbehave at all—until the next time, that is!

Most of the time, we do what we are told. Most of the time, that one eyebrow that Mother can so artistically raise so abnormally high suffices to warn us that we are about to step across the line. Most of the time, naughty behavior stops before it ever begins. We're sorry we didn't see Mother's eyebrow on this occasion.

After doling out my brothers' punishment, Mother instructed us, "Pick up every last feather that came out of that pillow. Mary Ann, you are a part of this, too." Mother turned abruptly and went downstairs. I wouldn't blame her if she had stomped her way down the stairs, but house slippers don't lend themselves to that so much!

Dale said, "I'll take my part of the blame. How about you two?"

Thurston complained, "All I did was see Kyle snitch your house on Boardwalk."

Kyle scolded, "It doesn't matter. We are all guilty except for little sis. And we got her into trouble, too!"

"I've never been so humiliated in my life," proclaimed Dale. "Glad our cousins didn't see Mother spankin' us with a house slipper. We'd be the laughin' stock, wouldn't we?"

The silence was deafening.

Without saying a word, I picked up the pillow tick to hold out for the boys to refill. Good thing the ticking was heavy duty, because we stuffed that pillow with feathers for two whole hours. How Mommy Laurie ever got that many chicken feathers into one pillow, I'll never know!

I don't think my brothers will ever have another pillow fight. I believe that picking up feathers from every inch of that dormitory might have been punishment enough. Feathers were even in the light fixtures. There was no more Monopoly that night! And I would have to seriously reconsider my job as banker in the next Monopoly game.

Kyle, being the oldest, announced, "Now, let's go on to bed. It's my turn to clean up the dormitory tomorrow before we go back to Emory. I'll just vacuum up any stray feathers I find. No one will ever know that we didn't pick up all of them by hand. Dale, tomorrow morning, you and Thurston take the bed covers and feather beds outside and beat them good to make sure they are clean."

Exhausted by what the night brought, my brothers were only too happy to comply. Our mountain probably won't see another pillow fight for a long time.

Lessons from Mommy Laurie

Our mountain can blow some mighty cold winds in the wintertime. Throughout the night, every night, Mommy tends the fires that warm our home! It takes a lot of wood and coal to feed the one-hundred-year-old rock fireplace, the Warm Morning stove, and the cookstove in the kitchen. During the hottest months, Mommy cooks our meals and cans vegetables in the summer kitchen. If we have a lot of quart or half-gallon jars of vegetables to preserve, Mommy uses a huge tub over an outdoor fire pit. Lye soap is made in a big cauldron over the fire pit, too. The cows get milked twice a day, mostly by Mommy. Then, there are the chickens! Any time she does sit down, my grandmother has socks to darn, torn clothes to mend, quilt squares to piece, afghans to knit for gifts, and pretties to crochet and embroider.

My blue jeans have at least five pretty red plaid patches on them. Mommy chuckled when I asked her if she would sew elbow patches on my jacket to match. When she heard that now all my friends want a jacket with patches and the fancy needlework just like mine, Mommy chuckled even more.

A couple of weeks ago, we made apple butter in the huge copper kettle forged by the local blacksmith. When apple butter is simmering on the open fire, it has to be stirred with a wooden paddle that is almost big enough for a rowboat. I'm not allowed to stir. The cauldron on an open fire can be dangerous for a shorty like me. Being short herself, my grandmother jests that she is as tall as she is around. But she manages stirring the cauldron just fine! I do help wash the jars, though.

Mommy tells me that my hands are just the right size to reach inside. I wash so many jars, I wonder if the size of my hands is a blessing or a stroke of bad luck.

It is three weeks until Christmas. I'm so excited. Mother will be home for the weekend by lunchtime today. She and my brothers will be home for good after Christmas.

Mommy spills the beans, "Your mother is bringin' home a surprise..."

I point out to my grandmother, as I often do, that it really isn't a surprise if she tells! However, that doesn't stop my grandmother. She asks, "You know how the coyotes got into the barn and killed all the cats? We need another barn cat. I think that maybe we will get a pair today. The Counts family in Meadowview has some pretty black-and-white mousers. They offered us two cats. One is male, and one is a female. Maybe we can raise some kittens. More cats will keep the mice out of the cows' feed bin. You know, though, you mustn't get attached to those cats!" Mommy cautions me. "It's like gittin' too cozy with the newborn calves. The calves will grow up, and your uncle Culley will take them to the stock market to be sold. We'll have no more tears over a lost cat or a calf that's taken to market. We will not name another calf no matter how endearin' those big eyes are. And I'll say again, I don't want any cats named, either. Do you understand?"

I'm thinking about the last calf, Lucy Lou—the calf we had to bottle-feed. Her mama died in childbirth from some infection. When she was born, Lucy Lou had to be fed every two hours. Trips to the barn even at night to take care of the newborn made for long, hard days for my grandparents. Needless to say, Lucy Lou went to market early, only to be bought for veal steaks to be served at Bennie's Restaurant over in Bristol, Tennessee. Lucy Lou's demise made a lot of people happy, I guess. Not me!

I think about the remains of Max, the big orange, black, and brown tortie that followed Mommy everywhere. I ask, "Mommy, why are you reminding me about crying over Lucy

Lou and Max? You gave Max his name. Max was your favorite cat, too! I saw you hide your face in your apron when we found him."

Mommy answers with a tight smile, and then she stares off into space. My grandmother is good for that!

"Mommy, do you think these cats will be able to stay out of the coyotes' clutches? Is Poppy still going to get a new mule to protect the cattle?"

"The new mule is comin' tomorrow. We're buyin' it from your grandpa Rose for only a hundred dollars. You know he raises the best mules in this part of the country. We've lost too many calves this year. Coyotes love to surround a cow that is birthin' and grab the babies as soon as they are born. Those coyotes are smart. They coordinate their strategy for the kill. The heifer is at a disadvantage and can't protect her newborn. We've already lost two calves. We'll confine the heifers about to give birth to the stalls in the barn. I have their birthin' schedules, but a body can't always go by that. And don't worry about those cats. They know where danger lurks!"

Knowing what happened to Max, I'm doubtful. I ask, "Do you think that one mule can protect all the cows that are birthin'? We're goin' to have six newborns soon, aren't we?"

Mommy explains, "A mule can be pretty aggressive. Just one swift kick can kill a coyote. The others will git the message that they need to be cautious because a mule just ain't afraid to fight a coyote. After a few encounters with the mule, the coyotes will find other animals to prey upon and leave us alone. In the meantime, it'll be good to have the heifers in the barn to make sure they are well fed and cared for. The mamas need to eat well right up to their birthin' times. We'll feed Poppy's sorghum molassie feed to the heifers. By the way, have you decided to go with Poppy to the co-op in Castlewood? It's time to git more sorghum ground up into cow feed."

Mommy really wants me to go with Poppy to the co-op this coming week to see what new gadgets may be waiting for us to buy. My grandmother does love new gadgets. Sure wish I could do Mommy's chores and let her make the trip. The yucky sweet smells of sorghum molasses wafting from the feed sacks don't assault her nose and stomach! It isn't any fun to have to carry a brown paper poke to spew in only to have to hold the poke all the way back home because there is just nowhere to pull off our winding, narrow road. And you can keep the molassie cookies for yourself!

If I don't go to the co-op, I'll miss walking around the farm supply to inspect all the neat tools and household gadgets. Mommy says there is an easier way to do any chore if only a body knows about all the tools out there in the marketplace. My job is to try to find a gadget that would make any job easier for my grandmother. Last year, I showed Poppy an apple peeler that screwed onto the edge of the kitchen table. He said to the clerk, "Now that's some contraption there. How does it work?"

The clerk took an apple and pushed the rod through the apple core. As he turned the handle, the apple turned and the peel curled off. The clerk asked if I wanted to try it, saying to Poppy, "It's even simple enough for a kid to do."

Needless to say, the apple peeler went home with us. Using the new gadget, I peeled apples for the apple butter last fall and again this fall. Mommy used her old paring knife, and together, we peeled more apples in an hour's time than ever before.

Mommy says that Poppy will miss my company on the trip to Castlewood if I don't go along! I'm afraid that I will miss more stories about relatives who came over from England on the ship called *Mary Rose*. That's my name without the Ann! I don't know for sure that this story is true, but I do know that stories told about relatives who fought in the Revolutionary War and in the Civil War are true. Poppy says some of our stories get changed as they're told from generation to generation while other family stories are in the history books. One thing, I know, is that I don't want to miss out on Poppy's stories!

"Do you think I could take along a Coke and some soda crackers on this trip to Castlewood?" I ask.

Mommy is only too happy to hear me say this. It means I will go. How could I disappoint my grandmother?

"We'll get some more Cokes from Miss Winnie's store. I'll make some soda crackers on the cookstove top the night before your trip." Looking one ridge over at twin spirals of smoke snaking up between the trees and into the open sky, Mommy announces, "Well, I see Ole Shep is back at it! He must have had some extra corn this year."

Curious, I ask, "Back at what?"

"You know, back to moonshinin', makin' white lightnin', as that clear corn whiskey is called. The bootleggers make it here in the mountains so the revenuers can't find them so easy. But that ain't nothin' we talk about with others. Whatever is their business remains their business. We don't interfere, and we don't talk about it to others. But our family don't hold to that way of makin' a livin'."

A revelation hits me square between the eyes! Every summer, trails of smoke spiral up into the air all around these mountains. Recently, I'd told Mommy that folks were sure doing a lot of canning. And just the other day, I told Mommy about a sixth-grader's dad sending Miss McCoy a pint of clear liquid to fix her cough. Snickers filled the schoolroom when the boy presented the jar to Miss McCoy. It was a mystery to me why the poor boy was being made fun of. After school that day, I helped Miss McCoy clean the classroom. While closing a window, I spied my teacher outside, emptying the jar in the grass. So, today, I think Mommy saw the opportunity to teach me about life on our mountain. Guess Mommy doesn't want me to feel left out. Guess she wants me to know what is going on around me. Guess she wants me to keep our mountain's secret!

Another thought smacks me on the side of the head. "Mommy, was that corn whiskey you added honey to for my sore throat and cough last winter? Why would anyone want to drink that? It burned all the way down to my toes!"

"It cured your sore throat, didn't it?"

I couldn't argue with her, but the cure was about as bad as the smell of sorghum molasses added to the cow feed. It was still a mystery to me why selling moonshine was against the law.

I drown my grandmother with questions. "How do the bootleggers keep it a secret if everyone can see those trails of smoke risin' up all over the mountains? Why do they want to keep it a secret? Why do folks like to drink whiskey?"

"Like I said," continued Mommy, "we don't talk about it to others. Besides, the moonshine is sold out of state. The moonshiners' rule of thumb is to not do business at home because it's bad for business. Talkers, don't-cha know? As to why moonshine is illegal—the Virginia state legislators don't think it makes for proper behavior of men. As to why folk like it, I hear tell that whiskey gives a little comfort to a troubled soul. Some even say that whiskey will cure whatever ails you. I wouldn't know about that—although it does help a sore throat, and Doc Caudill gave it to patients after surgery to dull their pain. What I do know for shore is that partakin' too much of the drink has ruint plenty of lives!"

"Mommy, do you think…?"

"Well, what I think is that we better git those apples out of the root cellar and make up several jars of applesauce. We'll use some for an applesauce stack cake for this weekend. I'll be glad to have a couple of stack cakes for Christmas too. What about you? While the apples are still in pretty good shape, we need to string some up to dry. Have to have those dried apples to make the fried pies for your lunch box."

"Sounds good to me! Are you going to make Kyle some tomato gravy to go over the fried chicken this weekend?"

"Well, I could make some off the bacon fat. Do you want some, too?"

"Mommy, surely you know the answer to that!"

Wild Thing Comes to the Mountain

"Hey, little sis! How's the world treatin' you?"

I answer my brother Dale with a great big smile. He squeezes my shoulder. I sure do like seeing my brothers.

Kyle, my oldest brother, looks me over and exclaims, "Little sis, I believe you've grown an inch since September! Come here, and let's see if your head comes to my shoulder."

"No way that's a fair assessment of my height. You are as tall as Poppy now. What are you eatin' anyhow? I hope it hasn't been Lucy Lou."

Kyle looks surprised. "Aw, shucks! What happened to Lucy Lou? Did Uncle Culley have to take her to market?"

"Yeah. Mommy and Poppy said that bottle-feedin' a calf wears a body down. They got her fattened up enough for the stock market. Some restaurant got some good veal, though. Mommy Laurie told me I couldn't name another calf."

"Well, I guess that's best. It hurts too much to lose a pet. You just have to remember that raisin' cattle is a business and each cow and calf is money for the farm."

Just then, my brother Thurston climbs out of the car holding a big box. Shredded newspaper spills over the sides of the box. Before Thurston can set the box down, a magnificent black-and-white cat springs out of the box and hightails it down the road toward the barn. It appears that the cat wants to escape the traumatic ride with strangers as soon as possible, while the docile black-and-white feline wraps itself around Thurston's neck and arms, most content to be held and stroked.

"Oh, no!" I cry. "How will we get that wild cat back? It doesn't know this place. It'll get gone and be eaten up by the coyotes! It doesn't know about those mean animals yet!"

"We'll fix that," consoles Mommy Laurie. "It's almost milkin' time. Christine, you're pretty late gittin' here, ain't-cha? Mary Ann, go see if Ole Cherry has made it from the pasture to the barn yet. You and Lassie round her up if she ain't headed this way."

So, curious about what my grandmother has in mind and not wasting any time, I head to the barn with Lassie, our faithful collie. As we hurry down the lane, Ole Cherry meets us halfway. Lassie barks her authority as she runs up to nip at Ole Cherry's feet. The milk cow looks back at Lassie like, "I'm goin'! I'm goin'! Can't you see I have a lot of weight to lug around here!"

Ole Cherry plods her way up the lane to the barn door.

Shoo-ee! Wouldn't you know it? That creature decides she needs to make a big cow pie right there in the middle of the doorway. No such thing as a small cow pie, you know! Ole Cherry continues to walk, chew her cud, and poop all at the same time. Amazing! How does a cow do that? And one more mess to clean up! I'm thinking that this would be a good job for one of my brothers. Not that I'm trying to get out of a job. It just seems we can't keep ahead of the messes around this farm.

I see Mommy and Thurston heading for the barn. Mommy is carrying her milk pail and a bucket of warm water. The docile cat still clings to Thurston as he and Mommy walk and talk. I'm thinking that this cat is not going to be a good mouser. It is just too tame!

Ole Cherry heads to her wooden feed trough. I scoop Poppy's special grains into the trough where the cow eats while getting milked.

Sitting on the milk stool, Mommy cleans off Ole Cherry's udder and teats. As Ole Cherry eats, she is very curious about this newest feline. Every time that cow turns her head and rolls those doleful, saucer-sized brown eyes to check out what's goin' on, she slings slobber from side to side. Ee-uww! A big string of slobber hits me. I'm telling you, on the farm, you never know what's going to hit you next!

Cherry's sac is so full of milk that it looks like she needs a girdle. Poppy put a girdle on Ole Jersey, the last cow we had! Ole Jersey's sac sagged to the ground when it filled up with all the milk she made. Cousin Clara and I joked that her girdle looked more like a monster bra! Overhearing this, Mommy told me and Clara to hush our mouths and act more like little ladies.

Considering a cow's not-so-perfect hygiene, it's important to keep everything clean when dealing with milk. Mommy uses a clean rag and warm water to do the first washing of the sac. Then, she wipes the sac a second time with mineral oil to keep the sac from chafing. After milking, Mommy rubs bag balm on Ole Cherry's briar scratches. Ole Cherry just loves to get into the briar patch left over from the blackberry bushes at the edge of the pasture. One has to wonder, "Just how much sense does a grown cow have, anyway?"

Mommy is intent on milking when, suddenly, a stream of milk soars up into the air toward the docile black-and-white as it clings ever tighter to Thurston's shirt. The stream hits its target. Another stream of milk hits not only the cat but also my brother. At first, I think my grandmother is playing a joke on my brother, but Thurston doesn't move; then, I see that he is wise to what is going on. Thurston and my grandmother always could talk to each other without ever saying a word!

Mommy picks up Max's old bowl and fills it with milk. Thurston holds the bowl to the feline's nose as he sets both down. It won't be long before Mommy teaches this feline to jump into the air to catch a stream of milk. Max was real good at it! Mommy loves to watch the powerful but graceful moves that only a cat has when in action.

"The cat drinks like it has never tasted such manna," Thurston announces. "This cat is the female. The one that ran off is the male. They're both good-lookin' cats, don't you think, sis?"

I agree, then ask, "Don't you think this cat's name should be Blackie since her head is solid black? Who would expect her name to be Blackie when she wears a silky white fur coat that even a snow bunny would envy?"

A frown crosses my grandmother's forehead as my brother says, "You do have a sense of humor, sis! I like the name."

Pretty soon, out of a stall comes the magnificent but wild black-and-white, casting his hooded eyes from side to side. He has perfectly-matched white socks on all four feet, and his eyes are as blue as a robin's egg. Blue eyes—not green, not brown. He even has a white M emblazoned on his forehead. That makes him special. Some say the marking is a trait that comes from the time Jesus was born. The story is told that a scruffy old cat made its way to the manger and climbed in bed with Baby Jesus to keep him warm. When Mary reached down to rub the cat's head to say, "Thank you," her fingers left a beautiful white "M" on the cat's forehead. It is said to this day that a cat with that marking is descended from that old cat that showed his love for Baby Jesus.

Wild Thing, a name I think fits him perfectly, nudges Blackie over and eagerly begins to drink out of the bowl. Mommy squirts him with milk as if saying, "We'll be good to you and feed you. No need to be afraid of us," but Wild Thing jumps back, bares his teeth in a menacing hiss, arches his back, and angrily thumps his tail on the ground. Just as quickly, he looks up at Mommy and lets out a pitiful little meow. Mommy aims another stream of milk at the bowl. Wild Thing gets the connection and slinks his way back to the bowl to eagerly drink the sweet milk.

My grandmother sure does understand nature. I don't know how she knows so much. She just does. Mother told me once that outsiders should never underestimate the intelligence of our mountain folks. Mother says there are many kinds of intelligences—not just book smarts. Mother says we should respect whatever intelligence a person has. Right now, I'm thinking Mommy Laurie is pretty smart about the nature of animals.

As we leave the barn, the two cats follow us back to the house. Wild Thing hangs back a distance, uncertain of what is going to happen next.

Blackie can't seem to let Thurston out of her sight. When we all go in for supper, Blackie stands at the front door and looks in. By the time we sit to eat, she finds us. Perching herself outside the dining room window, she stares at us as if to say, "Why won't you invite me in?" Blackie never takes her eyes off the action at the table. Whenever anyone looks her way, she stares back with beautiful dark eyes that say, "I'm still here. Pay attention to me!" Then, from her little bow-shaped mouth comes a prissy little "me-ow."

Thurston goes outside to scoop Blackie into his arms and to feed her a bite of table scraps. She purrs as she nuzzles him. I'm thinking I had better get out there and see if Blackie will come to me. I'm worried that when Thurston goes back to Emory, she'll try to follow and get lost. Thurston hands her over as he continues to stroke behind her ears. Soon, Blackie and I are friends. It seems she doesn't care whose arms she is in. As long as someone is stroking her, Blackie is happy. But what I really want is to be friends with Wild Thing.

Sunday afternoon comes, and Grandpa Rose walks the mule from his home just one ridge over to our farm. The men and boys take the mule to the barn for the night. The mule will be introduced to the herd tomorrow.

Back at the farmhouse, Grandpa Rose sits a spell and catches us up on the news about Daddy's nine brothers and sisters. That takes a while! Grandpa Rose enjoys his visit with us and seems to regret he has to leave. Before leaving, he squeezes Mother's shoulder and tells her how proud he is of her.

When Mother and my brothers head back to Emory, Blackie climbs my legs. I pick her up and stroke her until Mother's car is out of sight. I'm glad to have some diversion. Watching Mother and my brothers leave makes me feel left out. I wouldn't want my grandparents to know how I feel, because I love them and they love me. Mommy always holds her heart and says, "My cup runneth over with love for all my children, big and small. And there's always room in my heart for one more."

At suppertime, Wild Thing sneaks around. Mommy and I throw out table scraps, some for Blackie and some for Wild Thing. Wild Thing snatches up his scraps and disappears. It's going to take time for him to warm up to us. And I'll have to ease into calling him by his name. I don't want a scolding from Mommy, but I think that she will ignore me when I start calling Wild Thing by his name. My grandmother pretends to not hear a lot of things!

Mommy picks up the cat box that Thurston used for carrying the cats to our mountain. We take the box to the barn, add straw to the shredded paper, and set the box in the corner near the feed bin. Mommy says that the cats' scents on the box will make them feel at home and maybe, just maybe, this sense of belonging will encourage the cats to claim a permanent spot for a bed. Mommy is hopeful that the cats will get the idea that the barn is to be their home. I'm just hopeful that the black-and-whites will take a liking to our mountain and will still be here tomorrow.

Trek to the Co-op

With Cokes and soda crackers in a poke, Poppy and I make our way off the mountain to take the truckload of sorghum, oats, and rye to the co-op in Castlewood. It takes a big part of the day to drive there and back on these crooked roads. Then, it takes a while for the grains to be ground into Poppy's special feed for the cattle. We'll have plenty of time to look around the co-op for farm tools and kitchen gadgets. However, my favorite part of the trip is listening to the stories that Poppy tells about our family. There are lots of stories, and Poppy loves to tell them. Today's talk stirs my curiosity.

"Poppy," I ask, "just how old is Aunt Ellen?"

Aunt Ellen's birthday, or what we think is her real birthday, is coming up, and all the relatives will be gathering in to celebrate.

Poppy responds, "Aunt Ellen is nigh on a hundred years, based on the number of wrinkles on her face and the record of her birth in the old family Bible. She tells stories about how the Civil War came knockin' at her family's door right here on our mountain. Confederate and Union scouts were desperate to find food to feed their troops, so they confiscated vegetables from the root cellar, livestock from the fields, and canned goods from the pantry. Before the scouts could take everything, Aunt Ellen's mother sent her scurryin' off into the woods to bury sides of ham so the family wouldn't go hungry.

"About oncet a month, Aunt Ellen, ridin' Prince the big white workhorse, carried sacks full of corn or wheat to the gristmill. There, the grains were ground into cornmeal or flour. Sometimes, on her trips, she was halted by a band of soldiers. When asked which side of the war her family supported, Aunt Ellen would say, 'Which side you on? Can't tell too much about those raggedy uniforms. Really can't tell if them there are real uniforms.'

"If the soldiers announced, 'We're Johnny Rebs, little lady!' Aunt Ellen would reply, 'Me and my family is for the South!' If the soldiers announced they were Blue Bellies, Aunt Ellen tells that she didn't bat an eye as she shot right back, 'Me and my family support the North!' Never was her horse, her corn, or her wheat taken. Instead, the soldiers praised Aunt Ellen, 'That a girl! You know which side is right! Watch out now for those other soldiers, you hear?' You see, Little Chank, the mountain folk of Virginia were divided on the subject of war. Some Virginians in these parts fought for the North, and some fought for the South. Sometimes, brother fought against brother!

"For a ten-year-old, Aunt Ellen was quite the wise and wily one, don't-cha think?" Poppy says, sounding real proud of his relative.

Agreeing with Poppy and feeling some pride myself, I answer, "She was smart, all right, but I think she was pretty gutsy, too!"

Poppy continues, "Even though her two older cousins fought on opposite sides in the Civil War, they never faced each other in battle. Still, Aunt Ellen declares that her cousins' efforts were at odds and served no purpose—no purpose at all!"

I question Poppy, "Why would soldiers even want to ride their horses into our rugged mountains? We have a hard enough time driving a car through these mountains. Weren't there bigger and better farms to raid near Abingdon? Miss McCoy said that two big battles were fought over the salt wells located in Saltville. It's amazin' to me how 2,500 Confederate soldiers sent 5,000 Union soldiers retreatin' back into Kentucky where they came from! Several hundred men died in that last battle. I know why the soldiers needed food, but what was so important about salt? Why would anyone fight over salt? And why did the soldiers have to come so deep into our mountains?"

Poppy takes his time answering. "Not too many places have salt ponds or wells here in the South. Saltville had a boomin' salt business long before the Civil War. Everyone needs salt to stay healthy. Durin' the Civil War, salt was used to preserve the soldiers' rations and to keep the soldiers' horses from dying of hoof-and-mouth disease. General Lee's cavalry lost a lot of horses from the lack of salt in their diet. So you see why there was a struggle between the enemies to control who got the salt.

"Why the scouts made their way into our mountains is another story," Poppy continues. "The answer has to do with your friend Cassie's great-grandfather. There was no better blacksmith or toolmaker around. His reputation was known far and wide. You see, Cassie's great-grandfather repaired rifles for both the Confederate and the Union armies. He had to be a sly one. He couldn't let the Johnny Rebs know when the Blue Bellies were coming to pick up their rifles, or the other way around. The pickup times for the rifles were set for different times of the month. It was a problem for Mr. Gilroy when the armies got desperate to have their rifles back at the same time. When that happened, Mr. Gilroy sent one group of soldiers to a refreshment house while the other group did their gun business. The first drink, I'm told, was on Mr. Gilroy. Some folk say that Mr. Gilroy was a moonshiner on the side and that he made whiskey right here on our mountain. Other folk say that he supplied those refreshment houses with the whiskey he made, so he was making money all the way around. Yes, siree, Mr. Gilroy was pretty slick. He knew those soldiers wouldn't stop at one drink! The partakin' of too much corn whiskey can make a man drunk and forgit his troubles. Your grandmother says that drinkin' men forgit their manners, too! Can't much blame those soldiers for wantin' to escape a horrible war that took its toll on everyone in our country. Folk still talk about that war like it happened only yesterday. Now, don't-cha go tellin' your grandmother I told you all this, you hear?"

"Poppy, Mommy already had the talk with me about the mountain's secret. What I don't understand about Mr. Gilroy, though, is why he would risk bein' shot for treason if word got out that he was repairin' rifles for both sides of the war."

"I'd given that some thought before. I think the scouts were so exhausted with war that our mountain gave them a respite. The soldiers were willin' to forgit their honor to their cause, so they turned a blind eye to their enemies and to Mr. Gilroy's shenanigans."

"Poppy, I think our mountain has a lot of secrets. How do you know which secrets to keep?"

"Little Chank, some secrets our mountain should keep, but others our mountain should tell. It's up to each person to figure out what to do with those secrets. Sounds like you have some secrets you're not too sure about. Just use your heart and that good head on your shoulders and you'll figure it out. This is a case where it ain't like following rules at school."

Gathering up my courage, I spill a secret to Poppy I don't want to keep anymore. "Poppy, one secret I've kept is about Dianna's parents. A few weeks ago when I delivered their eggs, I heard shouts and screams coming from inside the house. I thought someone was hurt, so I opened the door. Dianna ran to the door, pulled me back outside, slammed the door shut, and told me to forget about what I saw. She said that her dad was drunk again. She said that her dad has problems left over from the war. Poppy, I don't think that gives Dianna's dad the right to hit her mom. At school the next day, Dianna told me everything was just fine now. I didn't believe her. Dianna comes to school sometimes with dark circles around her eyes like she didn't sleep too well. But, she is always happy at school, and she is one of the best students. She says that school is her favorite place to be. If I walked in her shoes, I'd rather be at school than at home."

"Little Chank, I see you've already become acquainted with more problems on our mountain. Last week, Preacher Lawson took Dianna's dad to the veterans hospital up in Roanoke. The doctors there say that Dianna's dad drinks to forgit the war. When he drinks, he has flashbacks about the Battle of Okinawa. He lost some good buddies in that fight against the Japanese. That particular battle lasted over two and a half months. I don't see how any man can come out of war without problems. Yes, siree, Dianna's family has its problems right now, but maybe they can see some light at the end of the tunnel from here on. I'm awful sorry you had to see what happened. If I know you, you'll be a good friend to Dianna just like you are to that little redhead who lost her dad in the mine explosion."

"Poppy, it's not fair that my friends Judy and Dianna have more than their share of problems."

Poppy seems to be thinking on what I said, and then answers. "Life ain't about being fair, Little Chank. Life is about making the most of what it hands you!

"Well, we're here already. Let's git this truck unloaded at the dock. Afterwards, we'll go inside the co-op to see what new gadget we can find your grandmother."

On the way back to our mountain, Poppy and I hope that Mommy will be pleased with another hand-cranked ice cream maker. It seems that our string-bean gatherings bring in more and more folks each year, and one ice cream maker doesn't make enough of that cold, creamy treat for a crowd of people.

We roll down the truck windows to let the cool mountain breeze fan our faces as we sip on cold Cokes and nibble on Mommy's salty soda crackers. Poppy and I enjoy the silence as the road twists and turns to take us back home. For once, the odors from the feed sacks don't seem so bad! I tell Poppy I'm glad I made the trip. Poppy answers with a smile and a wink. Poppy's wink means he feels the same.

Wild Thing the Courageous

Mommy is up at 4:30 every morning. She usually lets me sleep until 6:00, when I get out of bed to help with morning chores and get ready for school. This morning, however, Lassie's incessant barking gets us all out of bed early. From outside, we hear a strange howling come from the barn. The mule is braying as if the world is coming to an end. Poppy grabs his .22 rifle. Mommy grabs a hoe and the oil lantern.

We hurry to the barn with Lassie bounding ahead of us. We stand at the barn door, listening to see what all the commotion is about. Cautiously, Poppy eases the barn door open. Wild Thing is standing his ground between the mule and a coyote. With ears flat against his head, tail thumping the ground, back arched high, and hair on the ridge of his back standing straight up, Wild Thing makes his intent known with his hisses.

Lassie barrels ahead and crouches beside Wild Thing. She growls deep in her throat with such menace that it sends shivers down my back. Mommy passes the oil lantern to me and raises the hoe into the air, ready to protect her loved ones—people and animals alike.

The coyote hunkers down in a crouch as if ready to leap on his prey at any moment. As he sets his intimidating stare on the mule, the coyote seems to be considering the odds that may be against him. Poppy moves off to the side and aims his rifle when, suddenly, the mule turns his backside to the coyote and gives the coyote a powerful kick. The coyote hits the wall and goes limp. Poppy shoots.

The loud crack from the rifle sends Wild Thing screeching and bounding up the ladder to the hayloft. The mule's breathing comes in quick snorts. Lassie refuses to leave and remains crouched, standing guard and holding her ground. Her bared teeth and low growl signal that she is still ready for a fight.

Mommy grabs the mule by its mane and calls off Lassie. Poppy lets off another shot. After making sure the coyote is dead, Poppy shovels the lifeless body onto a burlap sack and drags it to the outdoor fire pit. That coyote is no more!

Mommy inspects the mule. There are some scratches on its side. Matter-of-factly, she tells me, "Your grandpa Rose ain't goin' to like this. He prizes his mules and hates to see 'em git hurt. Bring me a clean rag and the iodine from the cabinet above the feed bin so I can clean the wounds. Rope the mule and hold him still."

After handing over the rag and iodine, I balance on the milking stool and manage to place the rope around the mule's neck.

Mommy cleans the wounds. The mule is accustomed to being groomed by Grandpa Rose and remains calm.

My grandmother is a wonderful nurse. Down in Kentucky, Dr. Caudill and his wife took in my grandmother when she was only thirteen years old. Dr. Caudill trained my grandmother to help with surgeries and to dress wounds. So, like a real nurse, Mommy pronounces that the scratches are not deep and will heal in no time.

When Poppy returns to the barn, Wild Thing cautiously makes his way down the ladder. He begins circling around and around Poppy's legs, rubbing a thank-you, I do believe!

Lassie goes over to Wild Thing, and the two rub noses. Sure don't see that too often with cats and dogs, you know? Cats and dogs normally mix like oil and water.

When Poppy returns to the barn, Mommy asks, "Did ya see any sign of rabies?"

Poppy answers, "No, I just think the coyote was a rebel. Otherwise, the pack would have been together, coordinating the kill. The coyote may have gotten kicked out of the pack. I hear the others howlin' down in the far pasture. Can't git the mule down there fast enough. Little Chank, you better git on back to the house and head out for school. Don't want ya to be late." Poppy doesn't want me to miss one minute of school. I really think he doesn't want to miss out on hearing what I learn each day.

I hurry back to the farmhouse, jump into my school clothes, grab my books, and pick up my Annie Oakley lunch box with an extra fried apple pie already in the top oval tray. Tomorrow, there will be an extra chicken biscuit. Mommy wants me to give these to Sturgis because his dad got hurt in the coal mine down at Lick Fork and the family is having a hard time making ends meet. Mommy says a boy can't concentrate on his studies if his stomach is empty. I'll just tell Sturgis my grandmother always packs too much for me to eat—which she does.

My cousins are walking ahead of me. That's OK. The quiet lets me think about the tales our mountain has to tell today!

'Til the Cows Come Home

"Mary Ann, hurry and put your school things down. Go git on an extra sweater under your coat and put your rubber galoshes over your shoes for extra warmth. You and Lassie have to go bring in the heifers that are about to calve. My records show it's near their time. In fact, it's time to keep the heifers in the barn until they calve. It looks like it's about to weather. I see snow clouds a-buildin' over the Clinch Mountains. The temperature is droppin' fast. Put the whistle around your neck. If there is trouble, blow one long and one short blast as loud as you can. Don't forgit the cattle prod. Now, hurry along!"

Lassie seems to always know what my grandmother asks us to do. Lassie barks and dances back and forth in front of me as if to say, "Let's get the move on!"

Lassie and I run down the lane until we reach a level patch of pasture. The hard part is going the next half mile down the mountain to Caney Creek and crossing the footbridge to the next pasture. With dark coming on, I can't get down that mountain fast enough.

Lassie and I are making good time going down, but coming back up the mountain with slow-moving heifers will be a test of wills. When I open the gate to the largest pasture, holding fifty head of cattle, I see that I really have my work cut out for me. I run over to the first pregnant heifer and tell Lassie to hold her there. I collect three more and prod them until they join the first cow, where Lassie holds all four in one spot. The fifth cow has separated herself from all the others. I have to go to the far end of the pasture before finding her. I herd the heifer to Lassie and order her to take all the heifers to the barn. Lassie runs circles around the group and barks to keep them moving. Despite the urgency in Lassie's barks, the heifers slowly plod their way to the upper pasture.

"Where in the world is that sixth cow?" I wonder. "Why weren't all the heifers headed for the feeding shed like the others? Didn't they know there is weather a-stir, or were they already separating themselves from the herd in order to calve?"

I hear a sorrowful moo and follow the sound. Precious minutes pass before I find the sixth cow with a newborn. Things don't look just right. The mama is tearing the milky-looking membrane off the newborn. Cleaning up her baby seems to be taking a lot of energy out of this new mother. The county veterinarian thought all was well with the mamas-to-be, but apparently all is not well.

I'm really worried, but there is nothing I can do about the mama and baby right now. I need to help Lassie get the other heifers to the barn. Cold numbs my face. Fear takes hold. I blow the whistle one long and one short blast to let Mommy know there is a problem. Pausing between blasts, I repeat the blasts a couple more times. Mommy whistles back to let me know that she hears me.

Lassie does her job well. Watching her sets my fears aside. Ahead of me, she keeps four heifers in a group and herds them to the barn while I bring up the rear with a straggler. I gently prod the heifer because she acts as if walking up that mountain is the hardest thing in the world to do right now. She is carrying a lot of extra weight with her first baby. Since they have never given birth before, heifers seem to have a harder time than do dams.

Mommy is waiting at the barn, and as the heifers enter, she guides each one into individual stalls. Mommy talks as she works the heifers, "Raffer and Culley sent their workers home before the sleet turned the roads into a solid sheet of ice. Culley stopped at the barn. He went on home to give Lennie a call, but he'll be right back. Raffer is gittin' the tractor."

I inform Mommy, "One heifer is behind the blackberry bushes, and she has calved already. She was tryin' to clean up her baby, but she can't hold her head up. The baby will die if it doesn't start suckling. With the mama sick, the calf can't get its first milk. That newborn has to have the antibodies and nutrients from the colostrum to survive. And I couldn't do anything to help either of 'em."

I turn away from Mommy to hide the tears that make some of the boys at school tease me. Uncle Raffer is standing there. I'm embarrassed.

Uncle Raffer says, "It's hard to see a sick animal, ain't it? Mary Ann, I need for you to ride the tractor down the mountain and show me where to find the heifer. Are you up for it?"

Wanting to help, I answer, "That mama and baby need help. Let's hurry!"

Uncle Raffer attaches the wagon to the tractor. I haul myself into the wagon and think about how the coal dust covering Uncle Raffer's face looks like the dark that will be here soon. Uncle grabs the big flashlight from its hook on his lunch bucket and throws several chop sacks into the wagon. He climbs onto the tractor, and we begin our trek to the lower pasture.

A light sleet begins as we make our way to the lower pasture by following a dirt road that meanders around the mountain before reaching the bottom. It's the long way around, but the tractor can't negotiate the steep mountainside as easily as feet can. We finally reach the pasture where the heifer and her newborn lay. I wonder if we are too late.

The sleet stops, and snow begins to fall. What a strange turn of weather as Uncle Raffer and I approach the heifer and calf.

Uncle Raffer hops off the tractor and hurries to the new mother. Muttering softly to the heifer, he pulls on the heifer's head, trying to get her up. He goes around to the backside of the heifer, pushing and urging her to stand. I jump off the wagon to join in. That poor heifer tries as hard as she can, but she just can't get up on all fours.

"We'll have to leave the mother. Nothin' we can do for her now. Heifers have an especially hard time when the calf is a bull calf. Bull calves are always big."

Somehow, the newborn manages to get up on its lanky legs without any nudging from its mother. Uncle Raffer walks over to the newborn and picks it up to carry it to the wagon. I scramble into the wagon and kneel to hold the calf while Uncle Raffer rubs it down with chop sacks, then wraps it in clean sacks for warmth. Leaping back onto the tractor, Uncle Raffer starts the engine, and we begin our bumpy ride back to the barn.

Sounding a little worried that I won't be able to keep the poor calf from falling all over the wagon, Uncle Raffer shouts, "Are you OK back there?"

"Just like holdin' Lassie when I lift her up to the groomin' table! Calf's doin' a good job standin' on its own, though!" I shout back.

When we get back to the barn, Uncle Culley is waiting. "Need some help with that?" he yells from his truck where cousins Gilly and Patrick sit staring at the spectacle on the back of the wagon.

"Why don't you put the calf in the back of the truck?" suggests Uncle Culley. "Gil and Patrick will hold it. I called Lennie over at Mountain Aire Farm. I suspected there was a problem with the heifer and I knew that Lennie's dam lost her calf yesterday. His dam may be willin' to let this calf suckle. Lennie said he would rub down our calf with the same chop sacks he used on the sick calf. Just maybe, the dam will think our calf is hers and will accept it as her own. I told Lennie that he could have the calf for the effort."

Looking relieved, Uncle Raffer nods to Uncle Culley and explains the situation down the mountain. "The heifer is too far gone. She'll be dead before mornin'. Our vet is off to a conference and it'll take the vet from Abingdon too much time to come this far into the mountains to make sure the heifer don't have some virus. Better git it buried soon in case it is a virus;

we don't want a virus spreading to the rest of the cattle. I'm pretty sure it's just that the heifer was too small to give birth to this big fellow. In the morning, we'll borrow Delmer's small bulldozer to dig the pit for the carcass. The heifer is over behind the far stand of blackberry bushes."

As Uncle Culley leaves with the newborn, I ask, "Is there anything else I can do?"

Uncle Raffer smiles those white teeth at me. In the dark, his teeth are all I can see now except for the whites of his eyes. He looks like a raccoon with the coal dust streaking his face. "No, I believe you earned your keep today," he replies. "You better help Mommy finish the milkin' and git on back to the house where it's warm."

I enter the barn and find Mommy milking Ole Cherry. She asks, "Would you finish coverin' those two stall floors with clean straw? I've already done the others. Need to be prepared for the newborns. Cherry's stall was cleaned this morning. Take the other oil lantern for light."

Grabbing the lantern and the pitchfork, I set about my chore.

"I'm sorry that you're not real comfortable right now," Mommy apologizes to Ole Cherry. "Let's git that sac emptied before it busts. We'll be back on schedule tomorrow."

Ole Cherry is not any too happy that she is being milked in pitch dark. Agitated, she stomps her feet and swishes her long tail. The tail hits Mommy in the face and knocks her glasses askew. My grandmother is wary of getting kicked because Ole Cherry gets real cranky when milked off schedule. Mommy starts to hum as she milks. She says this is soothing to the cow. I think humming is soothing to Mommy. She sure does hum a lot lately.

Quietly meowing, Wild Thing inches his way towards Mommy when a stream of milk hits Max's old bowl. Hurrying to the bowl, Wild Thing begins to lap up the milk in perfect contentment. He stands and waits for another expertly squirted stream. Instead, Mommy picks up the bowl and squirts it full of warm milk.

When Wild Thing finishes off the bowl of milk, he brushes up against Mommy's legs. Mommy says to him, "I do believe you are a courageous one. Could it be that you're as brave as David when he went against Goliath?"

Wild Thing stretches his paws up to Mommy's lap and looks her straight into her eyes as if to answer.

Not fair! Wild Thing has shown affection for Poppy and now for Mommy. I catch myself so I don't speak my thoughts out loud. Watching Wild Thing, I wonder, "Just when, if ever, will you show me affection?" Then, I remember Blackie.

"Mommy, have you seen Blackie? Wonder where she is off to? I thought for sure she would be here by milkin' time. Of course, we're really late with the milkin'. This is the second day Blackie hasn't come for her feeding at the house."

Mommy answers as if she's really thinking on it. "Maybe Blackie is mousin' and just don't want any milk."

After finishing with the straw, I carry a bucket of water from the rain barrel to each stall. Mommy finishes with the milking. Ole Cherry heads to her stall where I left hay in the manger for the night. Chores done, my grandmother and I head back to the house, talking about the newborn calf, hoping the wee thing makes it.

Just one more day of school and we are off for Christmas. I'm ready for the holidays. I strip off my wet outerwear and stand near the fireplace. Sleep should come easy tonight.

Just before bedtime, though, Uncle Raffer, Uncle Culley, and my cousins pile in for coffee, warm milk, and fried apple pies. The talk centers around what the men need to do early tomorrow morning. Right now, they are worried about the mixture of sleet and snow. Sleet or freezing rain could keep them from getting to the feeding shelter. If the water in the troughs freezes, my uncles will have to use a hoe and break through the ice so the cows can drink. The cows tend to stay close to the shelters in the bad weather. They don't venture to the frozen creek in these bad times. It's important to keep the hayracks full in case we have to tide the cattle over for a day or two. Sometimes when the weather is bad, it's a couple of days before the tractor can safely travel down the mountain with fresh hay. Cattle need more hay in the winter since grass in the pastures doesn't grow as much this time of the year.

The men are doing some serious talking. It seems that the pasture is overgrazed. This is going to create a real hardship, because my uncles are not sure if we harvested enough hay for this winter. Poppy reminds my uncles that last year, we gave hay to the Dickenson family for their cattle. They promised to return the favor, so he gave Mr. Dickenson a call today. Mr. Dickenson assured Poppy, "I have more than plenty. Just tell me when you want the hay, and I'll even haul it to you. After all, you helped me out in a crunch last year."

That's the way it is on our mountain—neighbors take care of each other.

The men continue to talk about how they are going to have to divide up the herd next year and maybe lease some pasture from the neighbor who owns a ten-thousand-acre tract of land next to our farm. It's mind-boggling just to imagine owning ten thousand acres of land. The land was given to the Slater family in the 1700s by the royal governor of Virginia with blessings from the king of England. No one seems to know what favors the family did for this royal governor or the king of England to be given such a gift.

Mommy Laurie once said, "Maybe the royal governor thought he had nothin' to lose in givin' away this big tract of land since it was thought to be in Godforsaken country ruled by the Cherokee—land that no one else would ever want! Little did the royal governor know how rich the land was in timber, coal, and natural gas or that it would make the Slater family extremely wealthy!"

The dreaded discussion about burying the heifer crops up, and Mommy calls me to my bath. It's good to get away from all the talk. Getting out of damp clothes and into my flannel pajamas is good, too. When I finish, Uncle Culley is carrying a sleeping Gilly to the truck. Patrick follows, dragging his feet one in front of the other. We are all done in!

Uncle Raffer says, "Mary Ann, thank you for all your help today. You did real good. You stuck with the job you had to do first. Now, go to bed and git a good night's sleep!"

Embarrassed by the praise, I feel my cheeks burn. I wouldn't want Uncle Raffer to know how scared I was down in that pasture or how ashamed I am for crying.

I'm just sorry that Uncle Raffer can't rest yet. He still has a long hot bath to get, and coal dust to scrub from his hands and face. Aunt Tess is holding his supper in the warming drawer. He won't even get to hug Lizzie, his little girl. She will already be asleep.

Lizzie is the cutest little five-year-old you've ever seen! She has whitish-blond hair, big blue eyes that twinkle, rosy cheeks, and eyelashes that flutter like a butterfly's wings. We all spoil the wee thing rotten! Aunt Tess, Mother's sister, still calls Lizzie her little bundle of joy.

It will be hard for Uncle Raffer and Uncle Culley to get up earlier than normal in the morning to bury the heifer, and then go work on their knees all day, digging coal with pickaxes. Even though they own the mine, my uncles work right alongside their help. Uncle Raffer is the expert at setting the dynamite used to blast the coal so the miners can tunnel deeper and deeper into the earth. Uncle Culley installs the lighting, or else the mines would be very dark inside because the lights on miners' hats don't glow all too brightly in a pitch-dark tunnel deep inside a mountain. The other miners help lay new track for the coal cars. Every miner has a specialty. Every miner digs. That's just the way it is.

Uncle Raffer took me into the R & C mine one time so I could see some of the work going on. I wasn't allowed to go very far into the mine but far enough to know this was not a place I wanted to be. As short as I am, I had to stoop to walk because the ceiling was so low. I feared the ceiling would fall any time—it didn't matter to me how well the ceiling and walls were shored up with sturdy timbers! Coal cars rumble along the track and make the timbers vibrate. And vibrations cause things to move.

Whenever there is talk about cave-ins, I can't shake the worry that every day my uncles go into the mine, danger is lurking like the copperhead that bit my cousin Gilly last summer.

Tomorrow will be the last day of school until after New Year's Day. Miss McCoy has games planned to review the semester's work. She declares such Fridays as Fun Fridays! Even more than games, we all hope that Miss McCoy brings in the picture slides of France and of other places she has visited in Europe. Miss McCoy does a lot of fun things during the summers. Her father told her before he died, "Go out and see the world. Learn all you can learn. Marvel at all there is to see. Then, I want you to come back home to share this knowledge with your students while singin' the praises of our own magnificent mountains, the most beautiful place on Earth!" I know Mr. McCoy said this because Mother and Miss McCoy are best friends. And Miss McCoy does sing praises of our beloved mountains.

There has been so much excitement today that I can't fall asleep. I begin to think about what Christmas will bring. Christmas is in three days. The wall clock that my brothers and I bought Mother for our new home still has to be wrapped. My brothers and I used our allowances to order the clock from the Montgomery Ward catalog. It finally arrived this week.

On Christmas morning, we each will get one gift and our stockings will be filled with assorted nuts, peppermint sticks, tangerines, and oranges. I can almost taste the sweet juice of those Florida oranges right now. Oranges and tangerines are so expensive that we can only afford them at Christmas.

Some of my friends get a lot of toys and clothes from Santa, but my grandparents always remind me and my brothers that Christmas isn't about how many things you get. My grandparents say that "things" get used up or are soon forgotten. Poppy says the best Christmas gift is the gift of each other and of being together.

There is a lot to think about, and Mother and my brothers are coming home tomorrow. I start counting sheep. I count them every way I can count them—by twos, by threes, by hundreds, by thousands. There has just been too much excitement for one day! I feel that before I fall asleep, I will have to count sheep 'til the cows come home!

The Clamor and the Quiet

"Now, Lizzie, you just have to pretend to carry the Christmas cat that kept Jesus warm in the manger. You can't carry a real cat."

"But I want to!" Lizzie cries. "Ginny gits to carwy the baby doll. Penelope dwesses wike an angel. Patwick dwesses up wike Joseph in his wobe, and Gilly gits to be a shepwurd and carwy his cane! David gits to be the wittle drwumma boy."

"Well," I tell her, "you get to dress up in your real pretty bathrobe like a little child of Bethlehem. Do you want me to put angel wings on you and make you an angel instead, or do you want to be a little drummer boy like David?"

"I want to carwy the cat that Mary bwessed."

"But that happened many hundred years ago. That cat isn't here today."

"Yes, but Wild Thing has the M on his fwohead that Marwy bwessed him with, and I want to carwy him."

"Well, cats aren't allowed in the house. They are mousers. They have a job to do at the barn, and Mommy says we can't be spoilin' them too much. You will just have to carry your teddy bear and pretend it's the Christmas cat. Besides, Wild Thing doesn't like to snuggle." I wonder again, "Just where is Blackie?"

Every year all the cousins perform the Christmas pageant on Christmas Eve at my grandparents' farmhouse. We are practicing this morning, and my cousins patiently help with Lizzie. Finally, our practice ends, and we all look forward to when the whole family gathers in to have hot cider, molassie cookies, and applesauce stack cake.

Lizzie is spending the day with me today so that Aunt Tess can work at the grocery store over on Pound Branch. We finish our practice and, surprisingly, the sun is shining brightly and spreading its warmth. I decide to search for Blackie. Thurston will be real disappointed if Blackie is not there to greet him today.

After I bundle up Lizzie and lift her into the red Flyer, we begin looking all over the farm for Blackie. We check out the barn stalls. No more new calves yet! We climb up the ladder and look around the hayloft. Guess Aunt Tess would be upset with me for letting Lizzie climb up the ladder, but that little girl can clamber up and down that ladder as well as I can. I just hope that she doesn't spill the beans.

"What is Wassie barking at? I bet it's a great big bear-w!"

"Let's go look and see. Do you think Lassie found Blackie?" I ask Lizzie.

"I hope so. Let's go wook!"

We get to the corn crib where Lassie is barking. You never know with Lassie. Sometimes she gets excited at the sight of a snake. She wants to tease it, and then catch it by the neck for the kill. Sometimes she might bark at a bird that has just taken flight. Most of the time, we know when the bark is for more serious matters. This bark just seems more curious than serious.

I tell Lizzie to wait while I look farther under the corn crib. It would not be good if either of us got sprayed by a skunk or bitten by a rabid raccoon, so I am very cautious.

An adolescent bunny jumps up and hops with lightning speed out from under the crib. Disappointed and no longer interested in chasing a bunny, Lassie wanders on back to the house.

While we are at the corn crib, I decide to teach Lizzie how to shell the corn with the hand-cranked corn sheller. After all, I started shuckin' and shellin' corn when I was five. Poppy is always telling us children, "If you git bored, go down to the corn crib and shell some corn. And shuck some while you're at it. I bet your friends ain't never done that before." Now when my friends come up from town, that's the first thing they want to do. They like to crank the handle to shell better than they like to shuck the corn by hand.

Lizzie steps up on the crate so she can see down the heavy metal funnel with the sharp grinding teeth inside. After I caution her about the danger of the grinder chewing up a hand, she promises me she will do what she's told. Showing her how, I crank the handle, and the corn cob spits out into a barrel while the kernels tumble into a wooden bin. Lizzie is real smart and catches on fast.

After a while, we scoop up the shelled corn and put it into a partially filled chop sack. After a few more times at the sheller, we'll have the chop sack full. The old chop sacks come in handy. We reuse them for everything from holding grains to making dish towels and quilt linings; Mommy Laurie even uses the flowered ones for my dresses!

The temperature is dropping again. The clouds begin to build over the mountains, and the sky turns a steely gray. Yesterday, I had to walk to school in about three inches of snow. I hope that Mother gets here soon before a big snowfall catches her without snow chains on the tires. She keeps the chains in the trunk of the car, and my brothers know how to attach them. The problem is that in these mountains, a foot of snow can fall within an hour.

My grandparents are pretty good at watching the clouds and sensing changes in the air. I've even learned to predict that rain is coming when the thirsty leaves on the trees turn upside down and curl to catch water to drink. Poppy believes that the wooly worm can predict the kind of winter we may have. This fall, the wooly worm's stripes indicated we would have very cold temperatures and more snow than usual. Bad weather is the trickiest to predict in our mountains. According to Poppy, "It's like a bull. You just don't know when it's goin' to show its temper!"

Not many coal trucks are going in and out today, but I still have to look out for ruts in the road because I don't want to spill Lizzie out of the wagon. At least the trucks and cars that have gone in and out have turned the snow on the road to slush and I can see the ruts. The heavy coal trucks have left the road in a mess, and Poppy gets really miffed at having to haul gravel and ashes from the fireplace and the coal stoves to fill in the ruts. The Little Brushy Creek Coal Company running the mine down below us refuses to help maintain the roads. Furthermore, the great state of Virginia told my grandfather that despite the fact that this is a private road, we have to give everyone the right of way to their properties and the coal trucks must have access to the mines. Sometimes, I think that the great state of Virginia is not as noble as our history book tells us!

Lizzie and I get to the house just as Mother and my three brothers drive over the hill. Squealing, Lizzie jumps into Dale's arms as soon as he's out of the car. He gives her a great big bear hug. As he comes over to give my shoulder a squeeze, Dale announces, "Well, little sis, you and I drew the short straw for goin' after the Christmas tree this year. We better get started so we can get that tree decorated before the pageant tonight."

"Where are the cats?" Thurston asks.

I don't have the heart to tell Thurston that Blackie is missing. Instead, I tell him, "Maybe the cats are down at the barn. Who is going to babysit Lizzie?" I ask. "Aunt Tess is working at the grocery store until later today."

Kyle says, "Lizzie and I will find something to do, won't we, little pip-squeak? I'll bet we can find some blocks and build us a stable for the Baby Jesus."

Lizzie pouts, "I want to go git the Cwristmas twee with Dale and Marwy Ann. I don't want to play with bwocks!"

"Well, we'll get out the Christmas decorations and get them ready to put on the tree," Mother says trying to cajole Lizzie. "Kyle can get the bubble lights straightened out since he is very adept at that. And you can help string the popcorn for the tree. Won't that be fun?"

Lizzie responds with her name for Mother, "Aunt 'Tine, why do you use big worwds? What does 'a-de-pu-ty' mean?"

"Come on and help us get the luggage in, and we'll talk about that big word, adept."

Mother distracts Lizzie long enough for me and Dale to get the axe and head for the woods to find the perfect Christmas tree. Every year, we try to find a tree that's even prettier than the one the year before.

"What have you been doin', little sis? Did I sense that you weren't tellin' Thurston everything about the cats?" asks Dale.

"Yeah, we haven't seen hide nor hair of Blackie for several days. We're afraid that she tangled with a coyote. Did you know about the mule killing the coyote?"

"When Mommy Laurie called, she told us some of the story. It's too expensive to talk very long on a long-distance phone call, you know. You'll have to tell me on our way down the mountain."

As we trudge down the mountain, I tell Dale the whole story about how brave Wild Thing was in his encounter with the coyote. No need to brag on Lassie. She's always brave. It's a part of her training and a part of what's bred into collies like her. I tell Dale about the big debate Poppy is having with the coal company over doing its part to keep up our road. Dale is impressed that Poppy talked with our state legislator about how the great state of Virginia is failing its citizens.

Snow begins to fall. Within thirty minutes, Mother Nature gives us another inch of snow on top of the slush already covering the ground.

Dale says, "Boy, this would make a good path for the sled. Let's remember this side of the mountain. If it snows some more, we can do some real sleddin' here. It'll take a good twenty minutes to walk the sled back up the hill. It'll be worth it, though, don't-cha think?"

When I remind Dale that I usually get only one ride down the hill with them, he says, "Well, we'll have to fix that. I don't think Mother will let you ride by yourself, though."

Mother doesn't always allow me to sled with the boys. She says they are too daring. She has already warned them they were to never build another snow tunnel to sled through. When Mother saw last year's igloo with the tunnel through it, she looked like she just might pass out. Luckily, there were no broken necks or bones—just a few bruises. When the snow pack is good, the older neighbor kids and cousins sled with my brothers the entire day.

Poppy put an end to sledding down Rocky Bank. One time, the neighbors had to park at the bottom because the boys had packed the snow into an Alaskan glacier. The neighbors were not happy one bit. It took almost a week for the snow to get crunchy enough for the snow chains on the car tires to get a grip.

Dale and I finally reach the stand of Christmas trees that Poppy keeps planted in a clearing in the woods. Dale and I stop and listen to the silence. The snow is lightly falling. The Earth is so hushed, I hear my own heartbeat. Being in the woods during a snowfall is my favorite thing in the whole world to do. It makes me feel that the whole Earth is at peace and nothing bad can ever happen. I'd come here every day if I could.

Dale breaks the silence. "Well, little sis, we had better find a tree before we get snowed in. Those snowflakes are gettin' bigger by the minute, and it's beginnin' to lay on the tree branches pretty good. It looks like this is goin' to be a heavy, wet snow. We better get busy!"

"Over there is a pretty tree. Is it too tall for the living room?" I ask Dale.

"Well, it can't be taller than I am. About six feet or a little shorter would do. Let me stand beside it, and you tell me if it is the right size."

"It's the right size, and it's skinny. That will make Mommy happy because we don't have all that much room for a fat tree." I am happy with our choice.

Dale begins to chop. He asks me to pull one of the branches away from the trunk to make his job easier.

When the tree is down, Dale and I each grab a big branch near the trunk and start lugging the tree on the twenty-five-minute trip up the mountain and home. Because of snowdrifts, we can't always tell how deep the snow is in some places. We keep losing our footing only to pull ourselves up again and again out of what sometimes seems to be a tub of thick molasses.

"Little sis, I didn't know you had those muscles. For a little thing, you sure are carryin' your part of the load!"

"Well, I do a lot of work on the farm to help out. Mommy and Poppy work hard. Sometimes I think they work harder than most folks I know. But I am ready for a breather. Could we stop for a rest? I hate to squash your praise, but this tree is gettin' heavier by the minute and I need to get the snow out of my galoshes."

Dale replies, "Just for a minute. I think we are in for a really deep snow."

As Dale looks up at the sky, I can tell he is concerned. I remove the snow from the top of my galoshes. Even with gloves, my fingers are getting numb.

By the time we finally get the tree to the porch and knock off the wet snow, we can't even see the first ridge over from ours because of the blinding snow. Getting to the warmth of the fireplace can't come soon enough! We won't have much time to tarry in the warmth, as there are jobs still left to do before the family gathering tonight.

Charity

"Aunt 'Tine, let me put the angwel on top of the twee. Wet me! Wet me!" begs Lizzie.

Kyle lifts Lizzie up so high that she has to reach down to put the beautiful angel on the top of the tree.

"She is boo-ti-ful! Aunt 'Tine, ain't she boo-ti-ful?!"

Mother gives Lizzie a big hug and kiss. "Of course she is beautiful! And so are you! Now, let's get into the kitchen and get those goodies ready for tonight's Christmas pageant."

Mommy and Thurston shovel out the chicken houses while Kyle and Dale feed the heifers and milk Ole Cherry. I clean and box the eggs for D & S Supermarket in town.

"Stuart will be up to git 'em within the hour. Just hope his Jeep can tackle the snow," Mommy worries. She and Thurston join me. We set up an assembly line to get the eggs packed even faster.

Stuart arrives on schedule. "Laurie, the snow is gittin' pretty deep. Rock House Road is goin' to become impassable in an hour or two. Hope all of your family is home safe and sound," declares Stuart.

Mommy answers, "Christine and her boys made it in good time. The R & C Mine closed down early today to give the workers some time with their families for Christmas Eve. Tess made it home just a few minutes ago. You know, Monroe takes on small jobs when he's waitin' on supplies to come for bigger jobs. He finished the Stouts's kitchen today, and they are moving in right now. Shore is going to be hard on 'em in this weather.

"Where there's a will, there's a way!" proclaims Stuart. "Thanks for the extra eggs. You know folks want their eggs no matter what. I'll guarantee you that there will be several waitin' at the store right now for these eggs despite the snow. Everyone was doin' their Christmas bakin' this week. I didn't have a single egg left. Now my customers need eggs for breakfast. In addition, I have a couple of families I give eggs to as a goodwill gesture. You know, Franklin's son got his leg crushed in a small cave-in at the Lick Fork Mine. I'll have to remember to have you save me more eggs next year. It's disturbing to see families that are hard up. Laurie, thank you."

"You're a kind man, Stuart. That's one reason you have a good business. Word gets around. You're the only big store around where folk can still buy on credit and pay at the end of the month."

"Thank you for those kind words. The best to you and yours, Laurie."

Mommy comes out to the utility room. Turning to me and Thurston, she says, "Now you two get the little red Flyer, load up these eggs, and take 'em to the McClure and Wilkes families. They'll be needin' these for their Christmas-mornin' breakfast. Tell them, 'Merry Christmas,' and they don't owe us anything because the stores didn't need all our eggs this week and I don't want the eggs to go bad."

Our trip of about thirty minutes becomes a much longer trip because of the blinding snow. On the way back home after delivering the eggs, Thurston and I struggle with the wagon, pulling it through snow that is growing deeper and deeper. We have a hard time standing upright going up the last hill. In fact, we practically climb Rocky Bank with one hand on the ground for balance. Thurston jokes that we put a monkey to shame.

He says, "I sure hope I get a pair of gloves that fit my hands and a new toboggan for my Christmas present. I doubt Mother can buy me a new pair of jeans right now, but these 'high waters' make me the laughin' stock at school. Kyle and Dale's hand-me-downs are too short for me. My legs and arms are already longer than theirs. I'm ready to borrow a pair of Poppy's work overalls even if the kids at school do laugh at me. Mother says I'm growin' faster than a weed. Think she's right."

I look over at Thurston's hands. He hasn't complained a bit, but his bare hands are as red as beets.

"Well, you're goin' to start the new semester at the high school in January. Since you will be livin' here on the mountain and workin' in the chicken houses every day, you'll need some good warm clothes for all the farm chores. Maybe you'll get some new clothes that fit," I try to console my brother. "I wonder if Poppy's old galoshes will fit you. You're goin' to need 'em, walkin' around here, what with all the snow, mud, and chicken poop! I, for one, am glad you're movin' back home. I don't care too much for shovelin' out the chicken houses!"

Of course, I don't tell Thurston that there have been several packages coming from Montgomery Ward and that Mommy sits up at night knitting. Every time I ask her what she is making, she just says, "A little Christmas surprise for the boys, is all."

Glad to be home and to have the trek behind us, we find more chores waiting. We sweep snow off the porch and shovel snow off the sidewalks. By the time we finish, we look like two hound dogs that have treed coons all night. It's a wonder our tongues aren't hanging down to our knees!

Before we go in, I ask Thurston, "Did you hear Mommy tell Stuart that she was givin' him all the eggs she had, yet she had dozens of eggs for us to take to the neighbors? I felt a little funny about not tellin' the truth."

Thurston replied, "Stuart didn't really have to know how many eggs there were. Besides, this is Mommy's way of being charitable. And you can't fault her for havin' us tell a little white lie to the neighbors. She doesn't want them to feel beholden to her. Mommy told me one time that being on the receiving end of charity is not a fun place to be. You know she had to go live with Doc Caudill because her mother didn't have enough food in the house to feed all her children?"

Secretly, I'm glad Mommy had us tell a little white lie! Sturgis Wilkes will have eggs to eat with his biscuits and gravy Christmas morning. Christmas on our mountain is full of all kinds of wonders!

The Christmas Pageant

Laughter comes from the living room. Dining room chairs have been brought into the living room, and the adults are enjoying hot cider and coffee. Yeah, some are even relishing the taste of molassie cookies while others devour the applesauce stack cake.

The Christmas tree stands proudly in the corner. When Thurston and I returned from our egg mission, the tree was completely decorated. The lights are now plugged in and bubbling with joy.

From the bedroom where we children are getting ready for the pageant, I hear my grandmother say, "I just couldn't nurse another calf. The time and effort spent on givin' Lucy Lou a bottle every two hours took a year off my life! Boys, thank you for takin' care of the calf. Lennie called today to say the newborn is sucklin' like it will never get enough milk. He thinks all will be fine. And don't any of you ever again allow Mary Ann to name another calf. It broke my heart for her when Lucy Lou had to go."

I'm surprised by Mommy's words. Mommy shows her kindness more often than she speaks it!

The adults allow us children to conduct our own preparation for the pageant. I am getting the wee ones in line for the procession from the bedroom to the living room. Everything is in order, and it looks like this is going to be the best Christmas pageant ever.

I guess you might wonder why we don't have the pageant at church. Our preacher travels from church to church. He comes every fourth Sunday to ours. It creates a hardship to try to include all the children from every little church up and down the hollers. Besides, the weather doesn't always cooperate, so we just do our own pageant at home. Anyway, it's exciting to hear all my aunts, uncles, cousins, and family talk, laugh, and tell stories.

I take my place in the living room and begin to read the Christmas story from the family Bible. We sing Christmas carols, and cousins enter and exit the living room just as we practiced. Everything is going perfectly. Last to come in is little Lizzie with her hair done in the cutest pigtails braided with new red ribbons. She is dressed in her pretty pink robe and is carrying inside a big towel a bundle that looks a lot bigger than her teddy bear did in practice this morning. Lizzie squeezes the blanket for all it's worth, and the little bundle begins to move. An angry and loud screech pierces our ears! Out of Lizzie's arms soars Wild Thing. He lands hard, and then scampers under the Christmas tree, taking with him glass balls, tinsel, and a string of popcorn.

Lizzie runs to grab Wild Thing, yelling, "Bad kitty! Bad kitty!" He dodges. Lizzie grabs his tail. He swats her hand, and Lizzie lets out a scream so loud, Santa could hear it all the way to the North Pole. Wild Thing makes for the back door. With ears twitching and tail quivering, Wild Thing claws at the window to the utility room, desperate to escape.

Mommy opens the door to the utility room. Wild Thing tears through the door, only to have to wait for Thurston to open the back porch door to make his final exit.

In his haste, Wild Thing jumps over a black wriggling mound. What do you know! There at the back door is Blackie, carrying in her mouth a baby that she lays down beside three other babies. She purrs as she lies down beside her litter. The babies are so new their eyes aren't open yet, but they feel the vibrations from Blackie's purring and squirm to find a place to suckle.

Mommy announces to everyone, "Looks like we have to fix our own manger for God's little creatures. Mary Ann, git some rags. Kyle, you and Thurston go git Lassie's whelping box from the summer kitchen. Dale, go git a pitchfork full of hay from the barn."

After Blackie is settled in with her new family and bowls are filled with water and table scraps, Mommy announces, "Now, children, it's time to let Blackie have her privacy. Let's go back and hear Christine read. Does anyone want any refills on the apple cider or cake? Who ate all the molassie cookies? Monroe, you didn't eat them all, did ya?"

Poppy's grin admits his guilt as he looks at Mommy with soft blue eyes that twinkle. You would think they were two teenagers sparkin' each other. I look away because it's embarrassing to see my grandparents act like teenagers.

We always end Christmas Eve with Mother reading, "'Twas the Night Before Christmas." Mother mesmerizes us with Clement Moore's wonderful poem. We don't want the poem to end, but it does. We don't want the night to end, but it does.

Lizzie climbs down off Uncle Raffer's lap and asks, "Will Santa come tonight?"

Uncle Culley answers, "He won't if we don't git all you little children to bed. I believe it's that time."

Christmas is already everything I dreamed it would be. This has been the most perfect night . . . except, I wonder where Wild Thing got to. Hope the idea hasn't entered his head that he doesn't want to live on our mountain any more.

Christmas Day on the Mountain

Only one more inch of snow lay on the ground overnight. It sounds like someone hushed Mother Earth to be still in honor of Christmas morning. Before our chores, Thurston and I clean up Blackie's whelping box. Blackie doesn't mind that her babies are being handled by human hands. In fact, she meows her appreciation. Lassie isn't standing at the back door as usual. Thurston whistles, and out of the dog house comes Lassie, stretching and yawning as if she has just had the most glorious winter's nap.

Thurston pokes me. "Look at that, sis. What do you know!"

From out of the dog house, Wild Thing struts to come alongside Lassie. The two offer each other a "Good morning!" nudge on the nose. Will wonders never cease!

Thurston sets out Lassie's food. Not interested in food, Lassie and Wild Thing push their way past us to get inside. The tails on both dog and cat swish back and forth in excitement. Lassie reverently goes over to Blackie to check out the litter. Lassie rubs noses with Blackie. As Lassie moves her head over the babies to inspect each one more closely, she seems to be saying, "Welcome to our mountain menagerie."

Proudly, Blackie looks up at Lassie as if to say, "Look at what I did!"

Wild Thing remains aloof but curious. Then, he inspects the litter of four. Afterwards, Wild Thing licks Blackie's face, giving Blackie his seal of approval. Of course, Wild Thing must be the proud Papa, because one of the kittens is his spitting image, white socks and all. I can't tell yet if the eyes are blue.

Lassie hears Kyle and Dale on their way to milk. She remembers her job and barks to be let out of the utility room. Lassie bounds down the road to the barn to earn her keep. Wild Thing remains with Blackie, lying next to the whelping box filled with his litter of kittens.

Not wanting to waste any time on Christmas Day, the men are already making their way to the lower field with a special load of Christmas oats. I can just see those cows delicately eating while slinging their sticky slobber onto the cows next to them. However, in defense of that otherwise rather dull-minded creature, I have to say that a cow has a sense of fair play and has some manners after all. A cow is not greedy, for it takes just enough hay at a time in order to leisurely chew and chew and chew in order to savor and digest this manna from Heaven.

Thurston and I head out to feed the chickens and collect the eggs. Unlike the cow when it's fed, a chicken squawks its protests, flaps its wings, and body-slams any other chicken that may get in its way to the feeding trough. In other words, feeding time is a noisy, chaotic feeding frenzy. Feeding frenzies bring on an extra mess of chicken poop!

While Thurston, Mother, and I clean, sort, and box the eggs, Mommy Laurie cooks a breakfast good enough to feed Queen Elizabeth.

Morning chores done, we all sit down for a Christmas morning feast: sausage gravy, fried pork tenderloin, buttermilk biscuits, fried eggs, hash browns, and big dollops of apple butter on a second biscuit for my brothers. My brothers' stomachs are bottomless pits!

Poppy says with a grin and a twinkle in his eye, "Christine, I shore hope you make some money teachin', 'cause these boys could very well eat you out of house and home!"

Mother answers Poppy, "That's why I'm moving back to the farm. I've been thinking. We're going to have to double the size of that garden. I'm making plans to raise extra vegetables and fruit to sell to the local stores. I've already told the boys we will add more grapevines and add a few more apple trees. Virginia Tech already has my order for domestic blueberry, raspberry, and blackberry bushes. Strawberries will grow in three different patches of ground right behind the house. The Counts family taught me how to rotate the fields. Did I tell you that Stuart at D & S Supermarket wants all the fresh fruit and vegetables we can get him? It's hard to get fresh produce in these mountains because it has to be trucked in from the Bristol or Roanoke wholesalers. Produce is already past its prime by the time it's delivered to our mountains, so Stuart will advertise our produce as 'locally grown and better than fresh'."

"Daughter, why does it not surprise me you have thought all this through? You always were a deliberate thinker. Your mother and I are real proud of you. It'll be our greatest pleasure to see you walk across that stage in May to git your college diploma. We'll shore be glad to have you and the boys back home. We're all proud of you—family and neighbors alike!"

My grandmother interrupts, "What is all this serious talk? With all this jabber, did nary a soul remember what day it is? It's Christmas Day! It's time to see what Santa brought! Dishes can wait!"

We all jump up from the table and race one another to the living room. Poppy takes his place near the tree to pass out the gifts.

The boys each get a new pair of blue jeans and several pairs of socks. From Mommy, they get handsome blue and green striped knitted toboggans with wide bands that double up for warmth. A shamrock on the bands brags of our Scotch-Irish heritage. Matching knitted gloves have real fingers in them, and leather is sewn onto the bottoms of the fingers and palms. Mommy knows that the boys will need serious gloves for the farm work they will be doing. Mittens would have been a lot easier to make, but Mommy always considers everyone's needs.

I'm real pleased for Thurston. The gloves fit, and he tells everyone, "Finally, warm gloves! And they're not too short! I hope my blue jeans are long enough. I'll be back. I'm going to try 'em on."

Mommy gives me a beautiful yellow toboggan with a great big pom-pom on the crown. It and matching mittens are to be worn only to school. Funny how I never saw any yellow yarn in the knitting basket! Mommy must have knitted late into many nights before Christmas. She does know what a surprise is, after all!

From Mother there is a beautiful stationery box from Thalheimer's Department Store in Roanoke filled with pretty papers, pencils, a journal, and a note. Mother wrote:

Dear Daughter,

You have been such a great help to your grandparents on the farm. I figure that you have more than earned a break from your chores at least once a week. Therefore, I will wash supper dishes for you any night of your choosing every week for the next year. I will have to beg off certain nights when there are test papers to grade or report cards to do, but we can substitute another night. I hope this will give you time to write in your journal, which I know you love to do.

Love,
Mother

How did Mother know that I wanted more time to write in my journal? I thank Mother for this most appreciated gift.

Next, Mommy opens her gift from all of us. It is a brooch with jade stones to wear on her Sunday dresses. Poppy gets a pair of long, heavy woolen socks with leather bottoms to wear when he is resting by the fireside at night.

Every Christmas, we get a family gift. Last year, it was the Monopoly game. This year, it's Chinese checkers. The beautiful round cherry board came with bags of brightly colored marbles. The marbles are so pretty that I hope none of the cousins snitch them for trade in a game of marbles. Poppy made sure that he carefully routed and sanded the holes on the round so that the marbles sit perfectly inside. The board's triangles are marked off in perfect symmetry.

Wasting no time, we choose our marbles and set up the game to begin playing. Chaos breaks out when most of the marbles end up in the middle of the board. There is not one space left for a player to move the marbles. The goal is to be the first to get all your marbles into the triangle opposite yours. I have to move some of my marbles one space at a time instead of jumping several marbles to advance toward my goal. Sometimes I even have to go up into a triangle that isn't opposite mine, only to have to work my way out of it in order to advance. I can't wait to play this game again. It sure makes one think strategy.

I remember that I left Wild Thing in the utility room. I go to let him out to take care of his business. His coat is beautiful and glossy, and he looks all cuddly as he lies with his back against the whelping box as if he is protecting his brood.

As I reach down to pet Wild Thing, he haughtily raises his head as if to say, "You don't have permission to pet me. Get away from me. Scat!" Then, he saunters to the back door to be let out.

From behind me, my grandmother says, "You know that cats don't like for you to seek them out for attention. They like to seek you out. That's just their way. Ignore 'im, and he'll start payin' you attention. Be patient. Let 'im take his time." Somehow, my grandmother always knows what I'm thinking and how I'm feeling about things.

"Now, let's heat up some left-over gravy and pork tenderloin for Blackie and Wild Thing's Christmas feast. That'll get Wild Thing back inside. I've just checked the thermometer outside. The temperature is droppin'. It's already below freezin'. You need to let Blackie out to do her business, too. Then, we'll get all the animals back inside for the night."

I can't help but notice that Mommy is calling the cats by their names! Guess the Christmas spirit works all kinds of miracles.

It's getting late in the day, and the excitement of Christmas Day is coming to an end. Poppy decides to go to the barn to check on the heifers. A long, a short, and another long blast from the whistle cuts shrilly through the still air. That means we all need to get to the barn to help because there is an emergency. We drop what we are doing to rush to the barn, only to find Poppy grinning from ear to ear. With Poppy's ears, that's one wide grin! We find that there are not one but two new calves. One calf looks like he has just stood up. His mother is already nudging him toward her teats for his first milk. We all laugh as the newborn teeters from side to side, almost falling over with each step.

"Yes, siree, new life is always such a wonder!" exclaims Poppy. Then, Poppy seems to remember that even he can't get sentimental. "Remember now, these calves go to the market. There will be no namin' 'em. Y'all understand?"

Mommy hurries back to the house to gather up the milk bucket and supplies. Poppy motions to the rest of us to remain at the barn. Upon returning, Mommy is greeted by new electric lights flooding the barn. In all the excitement, she had not noticed the new electric wiring or dangling light bulbs.

"That is Culley and Raffer's doin's, as shore as I am standin' here!" exclaims Mommy. "Now, when did those boys have time to do this? How did they git this done without my knowin' it?" Mommy stops as if thinking. "Kyle, that's why you and Dale did all the milkin' for the last few days, ain't it? Well, if this ain't some surprise! Children, I'll have to say that these lights are a most welcome gift!" Mommy dabs her eyes with her apron.

There is even an electric heater inside a metal cage hanging from the ceiling. Mommy begins milking Ole Cherry while Thurston and I replenish the water and hay for the heifers. Kyle and Dale begin mucking out the stalls. I'm glad my brothers are moving back home to take turns with clean-up detail! Ole Cherry will add even more of a mess since she'll be staying in the barn during the day until this cold snap lets up.

Chores done for the day, we all gather around the fireplace to rest and to talk about the day's surprises. Poppy proclaims, "Children, this is the best Christmas ever! We all had more than our fair share of gifts, but the only gift we ever really need is the gift of each other. Yes, siree, the best gift of all is the gift of each other! That is the most precious gift of all! Remember that for as long as you live!"

As he casts his eyes around the room, Poppy gifts each of us with beautiful soft blue eyes twinkling with tears. Poppy reaches for Mommy's hand, smiles at her, and winks. They squeeze each other's hands. That is their gift to each other every Christmas.

It didn't escape the attention of my brothers and myself that we each received more than one gift this year. Even though most of the gifts are based on our needs, not our wants, that's all right with us.

This Christmas Day, Poppy's words seeped into my heart and made it feel like singing a new song. I learned some lessons today. Most of all, I learned that things don't matter, but caring for each other does. That's just the way it is on our mountain!

Wild Thing the Adventurous

More snow fell through the night. Morning chores done, Cousin Clara and I tag along with our brothers and cousins out to the side of the mountain that Dale discovered for sledding when we went to hunt our Christmas tree. I take turns with Cousin Clara riding piggyback with whichever older cousin or brother is going down the hill at the time. I figure that my brothers will tire of taking me down the mountain, but they don't complain. After my fifth trip down the mountain, Lassie appears to play with the kids waiting their turn. I notice Wild Thing watching intently from his lofty perch on a tree stump, staring at the gang of us children in his usual superior attitude. Ignoring Wild Thing, I pet Lassie, who slurps big kisses on my face, as that is the only part of my body not covered in warm woolen clothing.

In the middle of the afternoon, Dale and Thurston announce that they want to head home and warm up with a cup of hot soup and the ham biscuits and freshly-made cracklings that Mommy Laurie and Mother promised them.

Kyle wants one last trip. He yells, "Little sis, one more trip down the mountain?"

As soon as Kyle's words are out of his mouth, I don't even answer. I hop on the sled behind him so fast, you'd think we were racing the luge in the Olympics. You see, the day spent sledding with a gang of kids is short. Everyone wants as many trips down the mountain as possible. There are fewer sleds than there are kids, so to hurry everyone along, we pelt the riders with snowballs. Right now, the snowballs are flying at me and Kyle from eight different directions.

With a big thump, a gargantuan snowball lands on my back. The snowball hits so hard, it almost knocks me off the sled. When I bump Kyle, he almost loses control of the sled as he swerves to miss a tree. Claws dig into my coat. I holler, "A rabid raccoon is on my back. How do I get it off?"

"There's no stoppin' the sled. We are nearing the fastest part of the track! Besides, it's just that crazy cat!" Kyle hollers back.

Suddenly, long white whiskers tickle the side of my face. Wild Thing is climbing up my shoulder for a better grip. Good thing I have on several layers of clothes, because Wild Thing digs his claws deeper and deeper into my coat as we race down the mountain. I begin to fear that the sled will sling him off, but Wild Thing hunkers down and actually seems to enjoy the ride. His lips are fixed in a grin as big as a quarter moon.

At the bottom of the mountain, Kyle and I hear all the other kids laughing their heads off. We hear, "Super Cat! Super Cat! Watch him go! He bounds from the tallest trees. He soars through the air with the greatest of ease! Watch him go! Look at that cat steal the show!"

Kyle declares, "Wild Thing may not be a rabid raccoon, but he sure acts like one! That cat is crazy for sure!"

I ask, "Do you think he has earned his name?"

Kyle laughs as he replies, "Somehow, you knew his personality!"

As Kyle and I get off the sled, I expect Wild Thing to scramble off my shoulder as quickly as he jumped on. But guess what? That wild cat clings to my shoulder for the climb all the way back to the top of the mountain. Is that a smart cat or what? Who wouldn't hitch a ride up this mountain?

I tell him, "You're very intelligent! Of course, you already know that, don't-cha? You just don't go out and announce to the world how wise you are, do you? You're sneaky, sneaky! You like to keep things to yourself, don't-cha? You like to get in on the fun, too!"

As I talk, Wild Thing begins to purr. I think he actually wants me to stroke him, but I keep my hands off. I don't want to chance insulting him in any way.

Back at the top of the mountain, as everyone approaches us to get a closer look, Wild Thing bolts to safety. Where does he find safety? Yep, that crazy cat hitches a ride on Lassie's back. Guffawing, my cousins start chanting, "Go, Super Cat! Go!"

Wild Thing just gives everyone an icy stare and hunkers down for the free ride home on Lassie's back. Unfazed, Lassie treks home as if everything is just as it should be—normal. What a sight those two make!

Back at the farmhouse, we find Mother and Lizzie involved in a sewing project.

"Wook, Marwy Ann! Aunt 'Tine is makin' me a new dwess. I got to stand on the chairw and be a statue so Aunt 'Tine could fit me. Don't you think my dwess is pwetty? Aunt 'Tine is sewin' on purple buttons. Wook at the dwess for my doll. It matches my dwess. We cut it out today. I got to help!"

"Hey, little one! You look real pretty in that dwess. Did you really help make that dwess?" teases Dale.

"No, silly! You didn't say dwess wight. Say it wight!"

Kyle scolds, "Dale, shame on you! You didn't say dwess wight!"

Lizzie pleads with Mother, "Make them talk wight!"

Mother smiles and scolds my brothers, "Now, boys, you need to use proper pronunciation!"

"What is pro-new-sha-shun?" inquires little Lizzie.

Just then, Aunt Tess comes through the door after a long day at the grocery store. She gathers up several dozen eggs to drop off at John's General Store on her next trip down Rock House Road. When she sees the dress that Mother is making, tears fill her eyes. "That is just real good of you, Christine! You have made my little girl so happy!"

After supper, Thurston and I tidy up the utility room. We gather up Lassie, Wild Thing, and Blackie to the warmth and safety of the house. As Blackie returns to the whelping box, she purrs to signal to her babies that it is time to nurse. The kittens knead Blackie's stomach as they suckle while she looks proudly upon her litter.

Wild Thing pretends he doesn't even know me. So much for his royal highness and any gratitude for a great joyride today! Lassie eyes the menagerie of cats and kittens to make sure all is well and then falls into a deep sleep.

At bedtime, Thurston calls out, "Hey, sis, I think you gave that cat the right name. He's a wild thing, all right!"

Kyle yells out, "Yeah, he's wilder than any rabid raccoon!"

"At least he gave you a lot of his royal highness's attention today. He'll give you the cold shoulder tomorrow," adds Dale.

As I go to the bedroom, Mommy Laurie is turning down my bed. She does that for each of us every night. Mother says that is her way to say she loves us. I go to sleep thinking how lucky I am to be a part of this Scotch-Irish-Cherokee clan. I'm so glad that the mountain drew my ancestors here to call it home.

Mountaintop Blues

It's New Year's Day. No sledding today. Mother's cousin Prater and Uncle Squire are taking their trucks to Emory to move Mother and my brothers back home. Mommy rises early to pack ham biscuits and freshly made fried apple pies for their lunch. Mommy stuffs a poke full of molassie cookies for snacks. Once again, I'm going to miss out on all the fun. I console myself that soon, my family will all be together.

Mother drives her car so that she and Thurston can stuff it full while the men load the trucks with Kyle and Dale's help. The furniture will be stored in an old outbuilding on the farm until my grandfather can add enough rooms to sleep four kids. Mother will continue to lease the farm and farmhouse where our family once lived. We need the extra income, she says. We also need to be close to my grandparents to help with the farm chores. Our farm is becoming known throughout the county, and Mother wants to increase its productivity and earning power.

Mother and Poppy have drawn up the plans for the new house. My bedroom will be the smallest. I don't mind. Mother has already bought me a new matching white desk and dresser set, and she let me pick out the fabric for a new pink bedspread and bed skirt. Mother says I can help make it. After all, I made my first chop sack dress last summer.

Dale and Thurston will have new bunk beds and a new desk. Kyle will get his own bedroom since he is the oldest. He will use the bed and dresser that Mother inherited from Aunt Neve. Kyle will be home only one more year, so he gets a lot of special privileges.

Mother has already begun piecing together quilts for the boys' bedspreads. Kyle's quilt will be a pretty blue-and-white plaid. Dale and Thurston's quilts will be several shades of brown trimmed with a dark brown cording. Mother makes sure we all get something special. Mommy will host a quilting bee, and all the neighbor women will come to get the quilts finished in no time at all! However, Poppy says he doesn't know which will get done the most—the quilting or the gossiping!

It has already been a long day. I miss my brothers' help. Poppy and I take the hay down to the cattle, since Uncle Raffer and Uncle Culley had to go into the mine early today to check the generators and the mine's air quality. Methane gas is a bigger danger to the miners than a collapsed ceiling. Methane gas can be a silent killer if it is breathed in, or it can explode at any moment and blow everything around into smithereens. Coal dust in the lungs can kill, too! My uncles seem to cough a lot.

Full production of the R & C Mine will start back up at ten o'clock today. Since the contract with the trucking company that hauls their coal runs out in a day or two, Uncle Raffer and Uncle Culley have to renew the service. In addition, they have to renew the land lease that gives them the rights to mine under the Radcliff farm. The coal seam they are digging is so rich that Uncle Raffer says it is as good as gold and will last another couple of years. This means food on the tables for a lot of families.

The tractor ride is a welcome distraction. Any chance to get out of the house is welcome. It is just way too quiet without my brothers.

Poppy reveals to me his plans for making the farm more productive. I get the feeling that my ears are going to tire from so much "productivity" talk in the future, but I'll listen to anything Poppy has to say. He talks to me like I am a grown-up. I like that.

Poppy replenishes the hay for the cattle while I climb up the mountain a good distance to the springhouse and get the hose set up to run water to the troughs. It's a good thing the temperature has gone up some, because that makes my job easier. Wrestling a cold, stiff water hose is like wrestling a stubborn Lizzie when she doesn't want to take a nap. Both stub up and refuse to go in the right direction.

The cattle and mule are in good shape. Back at the barn, Poppy decides we need to check on the new calves and see how the other mamas-to-be are faring. When we get to the barn, we see that a heifer has calved, probably shortly after milking time. Another heifer is in labor and the baby's sac is tinged in black. The baby's back legs are coming out first. The front legs are supposed to come out first. The baby's legs are lifeless. The look on Poppy's face tells me this is not good.

Despite the crisis, Poppy is calm. He directs me, "In the cabinet above the feed bin, you'll find shears that your grandmother has wrapped in butcher's paper. I have the feelin' the umbilical cord is wrapped around the calf's neck. Somethin' is cuttin' its air off. I may need to cut the cord."

As I lay all the items on the nearby shelf, Poppy says, "Now, go git your grandmother and tell her to bring the turkey baster, some clean rags, and another bottle of iodine for cleansin' the navel."

"Lassie, go get Mommy!" I beg.

I know that Lassie can get to the house sooner than I can. Already, the urgency in her bark will let Mommy know something is wrong.

By the time I arrive, my grandmother is waiting on the front porch in anticipation. I yell, "Poppy says to bring the turkey baster, clean rags, and another bottle of iodine. One heifer is calvin'. Her baby's sac is turning black. Poppy is pulling the baby out to try to save it. Hurry, Poppy needs your help!"

Mommy rushes into the house to gather up the supplies. It surprises me how fast my grandmother moves!

When we get to the barn, we find Poppy unwrapping the umbilical cord from around the calf's neck. Poppy leaves the cord connected because it acts as an air hose from the mama to the calf. He tears the sticky, milky membrane from around the baby's mouth and nose. He forces the mouth open, sweeps it with one hand, and pulls out goop. Grabbing the turkey baster from Mommy's hand, Poppy suctions mucous from the calf's nose. Holding the mouth and one nostril closed, Poppy begins to blow air into the other nostril. The calf's long spindly legs begin to thrash about, and it begins to breathe on its own.

Mommy cuts the calf's umbilical cord and pours iodine over the navel. She tells us, "That'll kill the bacteria that a warm, moist navel attracts. I'll leave the rest of the clean-up to the new mother."

We watch as the new mother cleans up her baby and nudges it to stand to take its first milk. This baby will now have all the antibodies it needs to live a healthy life.

"Little Chank," instructs my grandfather, "go over to the feed bin there and git me that jar of clear liquid. I need to clean this mucous out of my mouth."

As I hand the jar to Poppy, I know immediately its contents! He takes a swig from the jar and swishes the liquid around his mouth several times before spitting it out. He repeats this. Next, he takes one big swig and swallows. And then another big swig!

Poppy announces, "Well, if this ain't been one eventful day! I do believe we've had our share of new babies and excitement around this farm for one season. What do you say, Little Chank?"

"Well, I believe somebody better make sure the paddock fence stays up real good before that bull breaks through it again and goes a-courtin' one time too many like this last time!"

"Hee, hee, hee." Poppy's shoulders are shaking, he is so tickled. "Did you hear that, Laurie? I believe Little Chank is beginnin' to learn the farm business."

Somehow, the blues got swept away today, what with all the commotion caused by new life being added to our farm. That baster won't be used on another Thanksgiving turkey! And will my brothers ever be impressed by Poppy's actions—both with the calf and with the jar of moonshine! Poppy doesn't partake, you know!

School Is Back in Session

Today is Mother's first day of teaching at the high school. She is excited to see her old friends and to begin working with her new students. My brothers have already met the coaches. They are anxious to get started at a new school as well. My brothers and Mother take the car today, but on occasion, they will ride the school bus that takes all the high school students off Caney Ridge to town. I don't have to leave as early as they do because my walk to school takes only fifteen minutes while their ride to town takes close to an hour. This morning when I tell Mother that I feel left out sometimes, she says, "Well, next year, you'll go to town with us for school. That will fit everyone's schedules better."

Mother's announcement stuns me. I guess I hadn't given much thought about where I would be going to school next year.

This morning at school, I stare out the window, thinking about how exciting it will be to get to see my town friends more. At the same time, I am really going to miss my friends Judy, Cassie, Ling, and Savannah and my cousin Clara. Just as I begin to think about how complicated life can get, Wild Thing jumps up to the windowsill and fixes his beautiful blue eyes on me. I look at Miss McCoy to see if she notices my cat and hope that she doesn't shoo him away. Miss McCoy glances at me and winks. She isn't going to shoo Wild Thing away; she has five cats of her own! Instead, she announces recess.

I don't feel like going out to play. Instead, I work on my math word problems. Miss McCoy comes by my desk and pretends to check my paper as she whispers, "Got a lot on your mind today?"

I nod and lower my head to hide the tears that are like a thorn in my side. "Crybaby" is not a nickname I want!

"Well, you do have a lot to think about. So do I. Can you keep a secret for a short time?"

I nod.

"The school board has asked me to go to the high school next year to teach French and senior English. It will be a lot easier to work in town since my home is right there within walking distance of the school. I declare, every morning, my old Buick groans in protest when we begin the trek up this mountain, but I love this little two-room schoolhouse and the children it holds. You know, you children on this mountain have taught me more lessons than I ever could have taught you. I will miss you all terribly."

I manage to look up at Miss McCoy. She smiles at me in understanding. I am surprised by what she has to say, but it does make the knots in my stomach go away.

Miss McCoy continues, "You already know Kaylee, Lila, Faith, and Elizabeth in town. Even though she is older, your cousin Laura will be there, too. And Ella and Grace's family are moving back so their dad can help with the engineering needed over at the Lick Fork Mine. You will still see your mountain friends at church. Think of a new school as an opportunity to meet new people. I find meeting new folks a lot of fun. The more diverse people are, the more you learn about the world. That's a good thing, you know? Now, why don't you go take care of that cat? I do believe he wants to talk to you."

I walk around to the side of the schoolhouse to the window where Wild Thing sits, and he meows as I approach. From his perch, Wild Thing leaps to my shoulder. He rubs his head against my cheek and purrs. As I reach up to scratch him behind the ears, I fully expect a protest. Instead, he moves his head underneath my hand, begging for more.

"Hey, everybody! Come see Wild Thing. He's ridin' on Mary Ann's shoulder again!" shouts Cousin Clara.

Wild Thing remains calm and stoic until the group of kids becomes larger and noisier.

"He can fly down the mountain with the greatest of ease! He can leap from the tallest trees! It's a squirrel! It's a plane! No, it's Super Cat!" shouts Bobby as he reaches out to slap at Wild Thing to get him to leap off my shoulder. Instead, Wild Thing hisses and returns the slap.

Bobby hollers, "You crazy cat! I was just playin' with you!"

My friend Judy steps in and says, "Bobby, you got just what you deserve. You should respect the feelings of animals more."

Wild Thing jumps off my shoulder and scampers toward home. I don't think he will be visiting me at school again, but I do appreciate that he was inclined to pay attention to me today and that he actually let me return the affection.

Both Wild Thing and Miss McCoy make me feel better about things. Going to a new school may not be so bad, but I don't want to lose my friends on the mountain.

Mother Graduates

We are all there. We sit in excited anticipation to see Mother walk across the stage to receive her diploma from Emory and Henry College. While we are waiting for the ceremony to begin, Mother's cousin, who is the superintendent of schools in these parts, walks over to visit with my grandparents. They shake hands, and Mother's cousin says, "Well, Monroe, I tried to get Christine to stay here and teach Latin and English over at Damascus High School, but she seems determined to go back to the mountain and develop that farm into a little business on the side. Can't really blame her. She'll have kids in college before long, and a teacher's salary is not enough to pay tuition for one, much less four children. She's makin' the wise decision."

Poppy replies, "Yes, Christine has always had a good head on her shoulders. She has already talked to the agriculture professors at Virginia Tech, and they've given her a lot of guidance. They are interested in supplyin' her with some starter seed and plants. In return, she has to keep records for their research on new fertilizers, rotation of crops, and the use of insecticides. She'll be busy and is undertakin' a lot on her own. I'm still buildin' houses, and there is more business there than I can handle. Christine and the children will have to do most of the work."

"Well, she certainly has distinguished herself here at Emory and Henry. Considering all her other responsibilities, she has done well. No one else here has ever finished a degree in three years. Monroe, you and Laurie have been her bedrock.

Without the two of you, Christine would have had a harder time of it. I admire you as much as I admire your daughter. Now, I have to get up on that stage. I'm the guest speaker. What about that! Me, a big ole mountain boy, a guest speaker? I think that our mountain folks are goin' to shine today!"

Poppy reaches over and squeezes Mommy's hand. There are tears in their eyes. Mommy takes out her best embroidered hankie meant for show, not for use, and wipes her eyes and blows her nose.

Poppy says, "Christine didn't tell us that finishin' college in three years is such an unusual feat. That daughter of ours shore is full of surprises!"

"She always was the modest one. I don't think I ever heard her brag about any accomplishments. We are blessed with all our children, Monroe. Who could ask for more?" Mommy wipes her eyes again.

The piano begins to play, and all the college graduates begin their walk down the long aisle. We all stand to show our respect.

Mother's cousin gives his speech. He talks about how determination is as important as being smart. Somehow, I think he must be talking about Mother.

Mother gets her turn to walk across the stage to receive her diploma and teaching certificate. We all applaud bursting with pride.

After the ceremony, we head home. May brings much warmer days, so Mommy packed us a big picnic lunch. We stop by the John Douglas Wayside picnic area to eat. Everyone is in a good mood, and no one is in a hurry. The hustle and bustle of the day is behind us. Before the gurgling stream lulls us to sleep, we load ourselves back into the car and follow the crooked road back to our mountain home.

The School Year Ends

It's next to the last day of school, and everyone is in a funk. The superintendent came to the schoolhouse last night for a meeting with all our parents, grandparents, aunts, and uncles. Everyone is disappointed that Miss McCoy will no longer be at our little two-room schoolhouse. We still don't know who will take her place. At least Miss Kelly, teacher of the lower school, will be there another year.

With tears in her eyes, Miss McCoy gave a speech about the strength of the people on this mountain. She said, "I admire the tenacity and the desire of this wonderful mountain community to educate your children. It has been my privilege to work with all of you. In giving me your support, you have really shown your children that you expect them to work hard in school and accomplish all they can. Thank you all for being my employer as well as my friend. I shall never forget you."

Cassie's dad stood next and spoke. "Well, Miss McCoy, I suspect I speak for everyone here. When you first came, some of us thought you was spoilin' our kids too much. You see, a lot of us parents still believed that if we spared the rod, we'd spoil the child. We were afraid you didn't know much about rearin' young'uns since you don't have none of your own. However, you taught us a lot about raisin' our children. I remember in your first meetin' with us parents, you insisted that there were ways other than a good switchin' to teach a child. I reckon you have a good understandin' of human nature. You proved that words are a powerful tool. It shore has been a pleasure to see our children come home excited about their learnin' and wantin' to do extra homework. That's been the case with my little Cassie. And she would read those Nancy Drew mysteries that you bring up from the town library until midnight if we'd let her. Thank you for gittin' our little girl excited about learnin'. Thank you for talkin' to her about jobs out there that a girl can do as well as a boy. Thank you from the bottoms of our hearts."

Next, Garrison stood and spoke in a bold voice. "Miss McCoy, reckon I have a right to speak, too. Some of us kids were talkin', and we want you to know that we think you are the best teacher around these parts. In fact, if the truth be known, you are probably the best teacher in the whole state of Virginia! We want you to know that we learned a lot from you. Some of us boys even skipped deer-huntin' season because we didn't want to miss out on your interestin' lessons. Thank you, Miss McCoy, from all us kids."

There were chuckles and amens of approval. With that speech, the meeting ended. Miss McCoy stood at the door and shook hands with grown-ups and children alike. She thanked each one of us again for the joy we mountain folks brought to her life.

The Wonders of Summer

School's out. It's summertime, and the wildlife on our mountain is thriving. The coyotes are prowling around other parts of the county. A black bear keeps making its appearance. A panther has been heard but not seen.

Black snakes and copperheads love to feast off the mice in the hayfields as well as those in the garden. The hummingbirds return to nest in the big maple tree in the front yard. They suck the sweet nectar from the honeysuckle growing in the fencerow. Blackie and her growing kittens now live at the barn. The calves graze in the lower pasture with their mamas.

Lassie and Wild Thing continue to share the dog house and to faithfully perform their duties. Lassie still tends the cows, and Wild Thing delivers a mouse to the front door each day as if he were delivering a peace offering. I really hope that it's an apology for not giving me the time of day. I just let him be. He is still a magnificent cat!

The farm is abuzz today with the extra field hands Poppy hired to help get in the hay. This is the third and last cutting. Kyle drives the tractor that bales the hay. Dale follows behind on another tractor with a wagon to pick up the bales. The field hands toss the bales onto the wagon.

When the tractors return to the barn, Thurston lets down the grappling hook used to hoist the bales up to the hayloft where they are stacked until there is no more room.

When the hayloft and the shed are full, Kyle stops baling. There is so much hay this year that some of it will have to be stored in the fields. The workers use their pitchforks to throw loose hay into Dale's wagon. When the wagon is full, Dale takes the wagon to a good spot in the field where the field hands again use their pitchforks to stack the hay around poles. Tomorrow, they will work the other hayfield and do the same.

My job today is to follow the field hands with a big bucket of water. The workers enjoy dipper after dipper full of cool water straight from the well. Working in hay is a hot job!

As I carry out my assigned chore, I keep an eye out for the tallest haystack. Later, Cousin Clara and I will sneak out to the stack and take turns sliding down the steep slope until the stack begins to give way. We will stop just short of getting into big trouble. We don't want the effort to put up the hay to be for naught. We don't want the hay to lay on the ground and rot. We don't want the cattle to go hungry. We do want to have a grand time on the tallest slide around!

Poppy is waiting for oak flooring to arrive from Coalfield Lumber and Supply for the ranch house on Longs Fork, so he came home early today. Curious about how the work in the field is coming along, Poppy walks down to the barn, and satisfied, leaves the work to my brothers. He makes his way to the old farmhouse, where he has been adding more rooms in his spare time. Tonight, Poppy and Uncle Culley will finish wiring. Once we have electricity, Poppy will work at night and on the weekends to finish the walls and paint. Already there is beautiful yellow pine flooring that will be sanded and finished just before we move in.

My brothers are learning a lot of carpentry and electrical skills as they pitch in to do their part with the building of our future home. Poppy assigned me the job of "gofer." I go for this tool, that tool, or whatever is needed at the moment. Watching Poppy makes me think about those different intelligences that Mother talks about. I think Poppy is intelligent when it comes to building a house.

My cousins Patrick and Gilly are helping Uncle Culley as well. Even though Patrick and Gilly are younger than I am, they are already learning how to wire a house. Saying you are never too young to learn, Uncle Culley patiently teaches my cousins his trade.

During the day, I have several jobs. Thurston and Mommy Laurie now do almost all the egg collecting and chicken-poop chores. Mother and I work the garden with the help of anyone whose hands are not busy with other work at the moment. Kyle and Dale take turns with the milking and cleaning out the barn. Uncle Raffer and Uncle Culley take care of the cattle. Mommy, Mother, Aunt Tess and I can the green beans, corn, and tomatoes. When the peach truck from South Carolina comes along, we drop everything else to put up peaches. As the blackberries, blueberries, cherries, raspberries, and apples ripen, we make enough jam and jelly to feed the whole countryside. Mother already has orders from the local grocers and neighbors for her jams and jellies. Thurston and I have carried so many loads of produce up and down Caney Ridge that we told Mother the little red Flyer was going to need new wheels.

The most fun thing about growing up on a farm is when all the neighbors come in to help string and break the green beans. While bushels of beans get strung and broken, the kids take turns cranking the handle on the ice cream maker. This year there will be two ice cream makers to make that delicious vanilla ice cream made with cream from the milk that Ole Cherry gives. You can have ice cream topped with raspberry sauce, blackheart cherries, strawberry jam, peach jam—ice cream just about any way you want it! My grandmother is all too happy to use up extra cream to make our favorite dessert. More than that, Mommy is doubly happy to have all the extra hands helping us string beans. One thing I've never understood, though—just how do so many neighbors know when we have beans to string? Mommy does know how to make work fun! And the neighbors go home with a mess of beans to cook for themselves.

While stringing the beans, the elders tell stories of old times. Once, we learned how gutsy my mother was as a thirteen-year-old. Uncle Culley was eyewitness to the fact. It seems that she met up with a copperhead with two big humps inside its body coming out of the hen house. Mother ran to the farmhouse, grabbed the .22 rifle, and shot the head clean off that snake. My uncles quote Mother to have said, "That'll show that egg-sucking snake. It sure explains where all the eggs have been going lately!"

I was surprised to learn that Mother could shoot a gun!

There are only a few more weeks until school starts, and there is still a lot of work to be done before we all get involved with school. Kyle and Dale will start football practice before school even begins. Thurston will play on the junior varsity team and his practice begins a little later.

Today, we are already working before the sun rises. We all shuck corn and remove the pesky silk. Then, all the women cut the corn off the cobs, fill the dozens of quart jars, and pack them into the tubs for their hot-water baths needed for preserving. Today, my hands are glad for all the help!

Exhausted by the end of the day, we all sit on the front porch and watch until the moon and stars begin their nightly duty of entertaining us as we name the different constellations. Mother tells us the Greek stories that gave birth to the constellation names.

We head for bed early, as tomorrow will bring another long day.

"Sis. Sis. Are you awake?" whispers my brother.

"Thurston, what do you want? It's midnight, and I was—I repeat, I was—asleep! You're going to wake everybody up!"

"Get your robe on. Come out to the front porch," Thurston urges, still whispering.

I grab my robe and drag myself outside. Thurston is the brother always full of surprises. I've never been disappointed. As I remind myself of this, Thurston says, "Look! I saw it from the dormitory."

What a sight to see! Flickering lights cover the entire mountain. At first I think the stars themselves have descended on Mother Earth! Thurston and I step off the porch into thousands of blinking lights. The forest seems to be filled with hundreds of Christmas trees covered from top to bottom with twinkling lights. As we look up, it's hard to tell where the earth ends and the sky begins. Fireflies are everywhere!

"Beautiful sight, ain't it?" Poppy startles us. Thurston and I look at each other. We know that we are both wondering why Poppy is rocking on the porch at this time of night, but we don't ask any questions. "It happens every year at this time. It's matin' season. This is the most I've ever seen, though. What a sight to behold! It always takes my breath away."

At Poppy's invitation, Thurston and I join him on the porch and sit there in silence for an hour, watching this spectacular sight.

Poppy finally breaks the spell, "Well, guess we had better turn in. Tomorrow will come all too soon. Watchin' those lightnin' bugs is the most glorious form of entertainment God ever gave us mortals, don't-cha think?"

Thurston says, "Poppy, if you knew about the fireflies, why didn't you tell us?"

"I suppose I'm a little selfish. I just like the peace and quiet of sittin' out here on the porch all by myself on top of this mountain. There ain't nothin' like it in the world. No, siree, ain't nothin' like this mountain and all its wonders in the whole world."

Thurston and I are full of our own thoughts as we tiptoe back to bed. I just hope that I can go to sleep. The mountain provided more wonder and beauty tonight than I could ever have imagined was possible.

And the Cat Roars

The last of the raspberries is a welcome respite for me. I, for one, am glad that Mother and I won't have to replenish the straw mulch to keep the weeds away, or pick any more fruit. Working alone today, I pick the last raspberries—in fact, the last of any berries for the season. My hands are spotted with bloody pricks from those wicked barbs meant to keep predators away—including human hands.

Soon, Poppy will plow under the garden and let the earth rest so it can do its job of providing our family with food again next year. Mother has mailed her last records to Virginia Tech. Even though the agricultural school there provided Mother with new hybrids of domesticated plants, she still had to spend a good amount of money for tools and supplies. She barely came out ahead, even with good sales to the local grocers.

Determined, Mother plans to expand even more next year. We put more potatoes in storage this year than ever before. That means more potato eyes for planting. A whole new field will be plowed in the spring for potatoes only. A bigger strawberry field has been staked off. It looks like the plans to make the farm more productive wasn't just talk!

A commotion from down in the hayfield catches my attention. When I look to see where the sounds are coming from, my heart leaps into my throat, for I fear what may be happening.

"Lassie, come here. Come here, girl!" I yell. I should know by now that the collie's agitated bark means that she won't leave until her job is done.

Lassie's barking gets even more frantic. As I follow the sound, I find Lassie crouching as she jumps backwards and darts forward to the side of a copperhead's diamond-shaped head. A good three feet long, the copperhead has pulled its body tightly into an S shape and has laid its head low to the ground as if figuring whether to grab for one of Blackie's curious kittens or to strike Lassie with a deadly bite.

Blackie's kitten is fascinated with the snake and thinks this is all a game. It doesn't know to fear what seems like play. My knees knock as I try to figure out how to help both the poor little creature and Lassie. When I command Lassie to come, she doesn't seem aware that I am there.

Suddenly, a fiendish screeching sound fills the air. A black-and-white blur comes swooshing through the air, ears flat on its head, hair standing straight up on its back, and legs and claws so extended, they double the creature's size. With the speed of a lightning strike, Wild Thing lands on the snake's back with his killer claws. He hisses as he digs in! The snake slithers away so fast, it is hard to believe it was ever there. Lassie rushes over to the baby, picks it up by the scruff of the neck, and heads toward the barn.

"Mary Ann, don't move!"

I freeze where I am. I hear the sound of a hoe hitting the ground.

"Shame on you! You should know better! You know that where there's one copperhead, there are two! How could you forget that they travel in pairs?" Mommy scolds me.

"Guess I wasn't thinkin'," I say as I turn to see Mommy toss the lifeless body of the second copperhead away from us.

"This one was ready to strike. I just don't know if you could survive another snake bite. We thought we had lost you for shore that time when you were five. And Gilly was in the hospital for a month after the copperhead surprised him. You know Poppy couldn't do without his Little Chank or his little Gilly!"

Wild Thing rubs against Mommy's legs, and, what do you know, he begins to rub against mine. When I look down at him, I ask, "Was that the lion's mighty roar I heard from you today? You are some cat!"

He ignores my praise and heads for the barn.

That night at the supper table, the talk is about copperheads, Lassie, and that crazy cat, Wild Thing.

Poppy warns us, "Every time we clear the fields of hay, the mice love to feed on the grain that's left. The fields are goin' to be full of mice for a while. And those copperheads know it. I don't want any of you walkin' through the fields or the woods without wearing boots. I know boots are hot this time of the year, but better to be safe than sorry. And keep your britches outside your boots. That way, if the snake strikes, it'll git more britches than leg. Little Jack told me that he's been seein' rattlers as well as copperheads down in the woods. So I don't want any of you takin' chances."

"Poppy, isn't Little Jack afraid to go ginseng huntin' this time of year with all the snakes out?" I ask.

"Well, I guess you haven't paid attention to that snake catcher he carries with him—the long pole with a loop on the end? Little Jack catches snakes for experiments on antivenom and puts 'em in one of those burlap sacks he carries on his back. The ginseng is in the other sack."

I feel sick. I've seen those sacks. The thought of a sack filled with deadly snakes makes me run to the bathroom.

"Honey, you OK?" Mother asks a while later as she wets a washcloth in cool water to put on my forehead. "Hope you don't mind. I thought I had better check on you. You are trembling. Snakes do scare you, don't they? I can't imagine how you had the nerve to get close to that copperhead today. You were foolish, you know? I suppose that sometimes, being foolish is part of being courageous. I do believe that you, Lassie, and Wild Thing were all a little foolish today. I just hope Blackie's little one has learned a lesson to run next time."

I agree with Mother. I just don't want to see innocent creatures get hurt.

"Mother, you know that Wild Thing is really the brave one."

Mother nods and smiles her mysterious smile as we head back to the supper table. Sometimes I wish I knew more of what lies behind my mother's smiles.

Back at the supper table, Dale asks, "Poppy, why does Little Jack hunt ginseng roots, anyway?"

Poppy explains, "Ginseng is used for digestive problems and other ailments. There is some research goin' on to study how ginseng could be used as an anticancer treatment. Ginseng is valuable to Jack for extra income. He has permission to hunt in our woods, but no one else does. Don't be tellin' anyone about this. We don't want poachers sneakin' around and destroyin' the huntin' grounds. Poachers are greedy. They take all they can dig. Ginseng is native to this part of the Appalachians. Once the roots are gone, there is nothin' left to perpetuate the crops. Little Jack is very selective about diggin' only the mature plants while leavin' the younger ones to grow into the next year's crop. Besides, I don't want strangers trampin' through my woods. Hard tellin' what other mischief they might do."

Thurston changes the subject. He's good for that. To everyone at the table, he announces, "Poppy gave me permission to invite everyone to sit with him on the porch tonight to see a show better than the Fourth of July fireworks in town. You have to remember that it's Poppy's quiet time, so no talkin' allowed, OK? Let's hurry up and get all our chores done! How much work are we doin' tonight up at the old farmhouse? We have to get back here in time for the show."

We all make sure our chores are done in time.

While washing the dishes, my mind is full of the events of the day. Thinking about how we were warned not to spill the beans about Little Jack hunting ginseng in our woods, I can't help but wonder what other secrets our mountain holds.

Preachin' on the Mountain

The Sunday after the fourth Saturday every August, my family hosts a memorial service for those of our family who are buried on a hill overlooking the mountain ranges that stack up one behind the other for as far as the eye can see. The memorial service has been a tradition for over seventy years. Poppy jokes that all those buried on our beautiful mountain are already halfway to Heaven!

From the cemetery on a clear day, we can actually see twenty miles away to the little town of St. Paul. It takes a long time to drive there. Sure would be easier to be a bird and fly. A neighbor up the road owns a Piper Cub, and he offered to take me up to see the mountains from his plane, but every time he asks, it seems I have chores to do. Sometimes, I just think that Mommy tells Mark I have chores to do because she's scared of planes. In the beginning, Mommy Laurie complained that the noise from the airplane buzzing over our farm decreased the number of eggs we collected by fifteen percent, but after a while, the chickens became accustomed to the drone of the airborne buzz saw, and egg laying rose to where it was before the Piper Cub.

All week, we have baked cherry pies, apple pies, and applesauce stack cakes. Today is the big day. Before the crack of dawn, we begin cooking. Green beans, corn on the cob, mashed potatoes, fried chicken, and chicken-n-dumplin's are all on the menu. We bake biscuits and cornbread, prepare fresh coleslaw, and slice Poppy's special onions and tomatoes into an oil and vinegar marinade. Aunt Tess's friend will bring her homemade chocolate and lemon pies piled high with heavenly clouds of meringue. Aunt Sonia will bring the biggest bowl of banana pudding anyone has ever seen.

Relatives and friends come from as far away as Ohio, Kentucky, Florida, North Carolina, South Carolina, Oklahoma, Maryland, Michigan, Tennessee, and Texas. We never know just how many folks will show up, but today, we expect about seventy-five to a hundred people to come to remember our loved ones and to talk and talk and talk.

Preachers come from several churches. The singin' and preachin' begin about nine thirty and last the entire morning. Personally, I would be happy with less preachin' and more singin'.

Because there are no hymnals for the service, a preacher "lines" the songs. In other words, the preacher chants a line of the song; then, the congregation sings it. I kind of like that way of singing. Some songs are joyful, some are sad, and some are soothing. Mommy says that the sound of those voices echoing across the top of our mountain is a gracious plenty to fill everyone there with enough joy and peace to last until meetin' time next year.

At the end of the service every year, Poppy stands in front of the gathering and says, "Now, we want all of you here to come eat at our home. Laurie and the girls have cooked enough food to feed that herd of cattle down the mountain. We'll ask the children to use the tin plates and cups and eat outside on the quilts. We'll let the grown-ups eat at the tables. As you finish at the table, one of the girls"—meaning Mother and Aunt Tess—"will announce there's an empty spot at the table for the next person. Everyone is welcome to sit on the porch for as long as you want. If you want to walk back up to the cemetery and eat in the gatherin' shed, you're welcome to do that, too."

Cousin Clara and I are put in charge of dishes, a chore we don't always like. We work on the back porch where a long table sits against the wall. We have a slop bucket for the pigs, a dish tub for soaking silverware, a tub for soaking plates, a tub for soaking glasses, a tub for washing, and a tub for rinsing. Mother keeps us in changes of hot water and sack-cloth towels. Just when we think we're almost done, another load of dishes appears.

After a while, Clara and I decide we are famished and need to eat, same as everyone else. Besides, we're tired of washing dishes. So, when no one is looking, we sneak into the kitchen, fill our plates right out of the pots on the stove, and go join the other kids on the quilts. Some have been lulled to sleep by the slight breeze our mountain always gives us even on hot days like this. And some of the kids are talking—or, correction, one kid is talking!

In a real citified voice, a girl is telling the other kids, "You know, in Baltimore, we have real churches with spirals that reach to the sky. We have lots of modern stores, nothing like the little country stores around here. Our schools are built of brick, not wood. And there are at least three or more classrooms for every grade. I just don't see how you hillbillies ever get a proper education in those so-called two-room schoolhouses."

Curious to see what kind of creature the city has brought to the mountains, Wild Thing sneaks around the edge of the quilt and starts to sniff delicately around the girl.

As Clara and I sit down, the girl informs us, "Oh, my name is Prissy. I don't believe I have met you two."

Clara and I don't even get our names spoken before Prissy continues, "I ranked at the top of my seventh-grade class this year. My teachers have told me I am so intelligent, they can already predict I will have an academic scholarship to one of the Ivy League schools. Do either of you expect to go on to school, or will you just get married and have a house full of kids like all these other hillbillies? It appears to me that every family in these hills has at least four or five kids. I'm an only child. On the way down here, my father was telling me about this

Rose family whose daddy died and left four orphans. It wouldn't be so hard on their finances if their mother had only one child to raise instead of four."

Prissy asks, "And, oh, what is your name again? Doesn't matter. Your hairdo is really outdated. Girls your age don't wear pigtails anymore. You need to cut your hair like mine—in a pageboy with bangs. And what is that dress you're wearing? I've never seen that fabric before. And, really, a big bow tied at the back! You need to get to the city and buy more fashionable clothes!"

"Sounds like you need to come to the country to learn some good old-fashioned manners, Prissy," my brother Thurston, who came out of nowhere, chides her. "By the way, do you ever stop to take a breath, or do you just babble on incessantly without ever listening to a thing you say? My sister's name is Mary Ann, in case you really want to know. And we all like her pigtails just fine! Didn't your parents teach you to keep some of your opinions to yourself?" Thurston shocks Prissy speechless.

After what must be an eternity for her, Prissy protests, "Who invited you into this conversation, anyway?"

"Well, first of all, a conversation involves two or more persons. As far as I could discern, this was a one-sided conversation. I do believe you like the sound of your own voice. Here in the mountains, we think it polite to take turns when in conversation. What are your feelings about that?"

"Well, who taught you such big words like discern and incessantly?" a baffled Prissy says, still trying to have the upper hand.

"Just because we live in the mountains of Virginia doesn't mean we are ignorant. Although I've just finished seventh grade myself, I've been taught that education happens in your mind, not just where you come from. I read. I read a lot. Mother allows me to read J. D. Salinger and John Steinbeck. Have you read either of them?"

Prissy shakes her head to indicate she has not.

Thurston continues, "Mother and I discuss the books as I read. I'm learnin' that life happens no matter where you live.

"Mrs. Childress runs a book club at the town library. Mary Ann and her friend Lila have read every biography in the library. Haven't you, sis?" Thurston asks, not waiting for an answer. "Prissy, what do you like to read—Little Red Riding Hood?" smirks my brother.

"I don't have to tolerate this rude behavior," retorts Prissy as she stands to leave.

"I do apologize, Prissy. Guess we should call a truce. I'll drop the rude behavior if you will. I just didn't like the way you were talkin' to my little sister. And I want to clear up one thing. My name is Thurston, one of the Roses you were talkin' about. About the number of children in our family, my mother says she never had a baby she didn't want. By the way, just why are you here today? You're a long way from home, aren't you? You don't have relatives buried in the cemetery, do you?"

"Yes, as a matter of fact, I do. My father is the youngest son of my grandfather, Henry Clay Stanley. He knew Daniel Boone."

"So did everyone else you ask, and George Washington slept in more places than there were days of his life! Daniel Boone did travel just south of here with our friend Mark's relatives. Unfortunately, Daniel Boone died in 1820, long before Grandpa Clay was born!" quips Thurston. In a more serious tone, Thurston asks, "You don't mean we're cousins, do you? That's our great-grandfather. That's funny. I've never heard of your daddy before. What's his name?"

"Daddy goes by Hank," answers Prissy, who is obviously feeling a little confused by now, if the slight frown on her forehead is an indication.

"I'm just surprised. Mary Ann, that would make her daddy Poppy's brother, wouldn't it?" asks Thurston.

"More like Poppy's half-brother, who was born when Grandpa Clay left Grandma Nancy to live with another woman. I heard Mother and Aunt Tess whisperin' about it one time. I just didn't put it all together until now. Guess we aren't supposed to talk about it." I surprise even my brother with my knowledge. He's usually the one who knows family secrets and such.

Prissy must believe us, because her cheeks turn pink, and for once, she keeps her silence.

"Well, Cousin, let us introduce you to the farm where Great-Grandpa Clay once lived. Mary Ann, don't you think she needs to know about pigs and cows, especially cow pies? Cousin, this tour around the farm will add more knowledge to your formal education than you would ever think possible! Right, Mary Ann?" Thurston asks with that look of mischief I know all too well!

"We have to get permission from Poppy and her dad first. Remember, Poppy doesn't like for us to venture too far with visitors because there are too many things that could happen. And we're not to let anyone new to the farm draw water from the well. Remember the boy who convinced you he was strong enough to draw the bucket of water and he lost hold of the crank handle? That crank handle is dangerous. We don't want anyone else to have a hole in his or her cheek," I remind Thurston as I look at Prissy. "I really don't want problems for Poppy or for us."

Cousin Clara decides she will forego the tour. She says, "Y'all have fun, you hear? I'm goin' to miss those cow pies sooo much! Yum!"

Wild Thing perks up his ears and meows. Before I can stand, he leaps onto my shoulder and drapes over it like a purring mink boa riding the breeze. He is just too funny! I believe he may be getting friendlier.

Jumping excitedly around Prissy's legs, Lassie wants to be a part of showing Prissy around as well. She joins us as we begin the tour with the corn crib to share the fun of shuckin' and shellin' with our newfound cousin.

Prissy is huffing by the time we get back to the house. She isn't accustomed to all this tramping around. Despite that,

Thurston doesn't give Prissy a breather from his enthusiastic tour-guide duty. He is on a roll. He tells her, "This farmhouse is as old as the hills, almost. Did you notice how thick the walls are?" As Prissy nods, Thurston continues, "That's because the house was built of big logs from the timber cut on this very farm. Although the logs are chinked with mud for good insulation, Poppy covered them in white clapboard siding, making for even thicker walls. The house stays warm in the winters and cool in the summers."

Little Lizzie comes to stand beside Prissy and says, "You didn't see the show we had the other night. My daddy woke me up to let me see these bugs with fwashlights on their heads. They lighted up the whole sky. Do you know why the bugs have to wear fwashlights?" asks Lizzie. Not waiting for an answer, she explains, "The bugs wear the fwashlights so they can find their way to the moon to git their babies. Then, the bugs fwy back to the mountain to raise their babies. Wouldn't you wike to come back to see 'em?"

Just then, Prissy's dad announces that it's time to go. They are the last of the visitors to leave, and Poppy shakes hands with Prissy's dad and gives him a big bear hug, sorry to see Hank go.

When all the visitors have begun their journey back home and all our chores are done for this long day, we sit on the porch and rehash the news carried from all the visitors. Thurston and I tell Poppy that on her long ride home, Prissy is going to be asking her daddy some questions.

Poppy says, "That all right. We should have told you about Hank before now. Guess we thought the less said, the better. It shore was good to see my little brother today. It was a nice surprise."

Thurston says, "Little sis, don't you worry about those harsh words Prissy said. Sometimes, people are insensitive to others' feelings. Guess they have to walk in someone else's shoes to understand why folks are different. Besides, I think the tour of the farm changed her mind about some things, don't you?"

"Well, she did stop prattlin' on and on like a know-it-all, didn't she? Thank you, big brother, for stickin' up for me today."

"Any time, sis! Any time."

Poppy asks, "Now, Laurie, you didn't have anything to do with that story about the lightnin' bugs goin' to the moon to get their babies, did ya? Sounds like one of your stories."

Mommy grins at Poppy. "Now, you know I wouldn't fill a child's head with such a fool notion as that, don't-cha? I'd never do such a thing. I did think it precious that Lizzie thought the fireflies were wearin' flashlights on their heads!"

We all laugh. It isn't the first nor the last time, I'm sure, that we will hear such a story. We grandchildren pretend we never heard Mommy's stories when they get repeated all over the mountain and up and down every holler, but one thing's for sure: As soon as Mommy's friend Miss Tully hears this tale, it will spread faster than a wildfire. Miss Tully does love a good funny.

By bedtime, I wonder just how many more secrets this mountain holds and how many more stories it has to tell.

A New School

Ella meets me at the door of Mrs. Buchanan's classroom. We enter and find the desk we will share. We pull down our bench. Our desk has one big opening for our books, and it serves to hold the bench shared by the two students in front of us. We sit near one of the biggest windows I've ever seen. I see Elizabeth and Lila sitting on the other side of the room. They wave at me. The rest of my town friends are in the three other sixth-grade classrooms.

Mrs. Buchanan looks around the room as she welcomes us with kind words and a smiling face. She promises us exciting films about the world outside the United States, science experiments to carry out, and new math to learn.

Mrs. Buchanan begins the day with our math lesson by reading a Chinese legend about Grandfather Tang and a powerful king in China. It just so happened that the king was having the biggest and fanciest palace in all of China built. One wall of the entrance hall was being covered in square tiles made of precious stones. Grandfather Tang was the master at making and installing these tiles. His grandson was his apprentice. The king was never pleased with the grandson's work, even though the work was excellent. So irritable and so demanding was the king that Grandfather Tang's grandson became very nervous. He dropped one of the tiles which landed in seven pieces. That brought on the wrath of the king.

The king demanded that the pieces be put back together to make a whole again. Seeing that this was going to take some time to figure out, Grandfather Tang told the king that he would like to take the pieces home in order to repair the tile on his own time. That way, Grandfather Tang pointed out, the king would still have his services for the day. The story ends with the grandfather teaching the king a lesson about being kind. There is a lesson in geometry as well.

After reading the story, Mrs. Buchanan asks us to work with the person sitting next to us. Ella and I are partners. Mrs. Buchanan hands us seven geometrically shaped pieces of paper of different shapes and sizes. The first thing we do is to arrange all the pieces into one big square, or tangram. Mrs. Buchanan announces the value of one piece and we have to figure out how much the other pieces are worth from the known value of one piece only. Ella and I concentrate hard, and in no time, we figure out how much each piece is worth as well as how much one whole tile is worth. Mrs. Buchanan puts more values on the board. Ella and I get the hang of it and speed through the rest. As Mrs. Buchanan comes by our desks to check our work, she whispers, "Now, you two come up with some problems for the class to do tomorrow."

Ella and I come up with enough problems for the whole week, and just for fun in the time we have left, we record equalities and inequalities with the tangram pieces.

At the end of a good day at school, I walk through the covered walkway over to the high school to Mother's classroom. I clean Mother's board while she packs up her books and papers.

We head home leaving my brothers to practice football. They'll catch a ride home with our great-uncle or hitch-hike. I like these private chat times with Mother.

Today, a jarring thought hits me. "Mother, Poppy is going to be real disappointed when he can't ask me questions about what I learned in school. Living in our new house changes things. Do you mind if I go to Mommy and Poppy's house at night to do my homework?"

"You're right. We'll make time. Poppy loves to learn about your day, and I'll bet he'll come up with some new problems for your tangram puzzle."

Poppy doesn't disappoint. He comes up with some new problems. He challenges me with some equations. As I try a few, he teaches me that it is like balancing the pieces on a balance scale. That really makes sense to me. Poppy and I use the relationships of the tangram pieces to create some more problems that I can give Mrs. Buchanan tomorrow.

Poppy asks for a copy of the puzzle pieces so he can study them some more. He does love to learn new things.

If every day goes like today, I think I will like my new school. Best of all, Poppy can still solve math problems with me right here on our mountain, same as always!

The End to an Otherwise Very Good Day

Almost a month of school has passed. I'm learning a lot. It isn't all book learning, either. Twice a week, Mother allows me to walk down the street to the public library to return borrowed books and to check out books that the school library doesn't have.

On the way to the library, I see three boys from my class riding bikes up and down the street. Apparently, they don't have chores to do after school. Forgetting about the boys, I enter the library and am instantly greeted by the smells of new books, of old musty books, and of the old oak library tables rubbed down with lemon oil. Mrs. Smith's old cat, Whiskers, comes to circle around my legs in exchange for a hug.

"My Goodness, Mary Ann, when are you finding time to read so much?" asks Mrs. Smith, the town librarian. "You and your book club are going to soon read our whole inventory. Yesterday, I met with the librarians from Wise and Norton. We are going to start a book exchange program so we can swap books your book club has already read for books you haven't read. This will save all of our libraries money. Everyone wins this way. Hope to have some different reading material as early as next week. Tell your friends at school for me, will you? I've already called Mrs. Childress."

As I'm walking back up the street to school, the same boys from my class are riding their bikes up the hill and around the courthouse. I just know their names from roll call, as I haven't had a chance to talk to them yet. There are thirty-six students in my class. Sometimes it's boring while waiting on Mrs. Buchanan to explain math to students who need more time to get the hang of it. At times like those, I miss my old school and Miss McCoy. It just takes longer, a lot longer, for a teacher in a big class to help all the students. Miss McCoy let me learn with the older kids or let me help my classmates. My classmates liked the help. Helping my classmates made me think real hard about different ways to get the point across—kind of like solving math word problems in more ways than one. I'll bet that Ella and I could be good tutors if Mrs. Buchanan let us.

Again, I see the three boys ride their bikes behind the courthouse. Lost in thought about school today, I don't hear them come up behind me.

Stan yells, "Hey, Mary Ann. How you like goin' to a real school in town? Bet it's better than bein' in that two-room school on the mountain!"

I answer, "It's different. There's good to be found in both schools."

"What's that book about—Rapunzel with the long hair? How long are your pigtails, anyway?" asks Parker.

"Yeah, why don't you cut your hair to look like your buddy Ella's? Now there's a cute girl. Her bangs even swing as she walks," banters Carter.

"For your information, my pigtails are really French braids. That takes more time to do than just pigtails," I retort.

"Well, see ya around," says Stan as he jumps off his bike, reaches behind my back, and snaps my bra. To add insult to injury, he yanks on a pigtail as he vaults back onto his bike.

"Hey! What are you doin'? That's not nice!" I yell at Stan.

As all three boys take off, I hear guffawing. One of the boys shouts, "You're goin' to git in big trouble! Her mother teaches at the high school, and her brothers play football."

When I get back to school, Mother is coming out to the car. I scramble into the car and quickly pick up a book to read.

Too embarrassed to tell Mother what happened, I hide my face in the book and pretend to read so that she doesn't see the tears.

All I can think is, "What will happen when I see those boys at school tomorrow?"

Later, as I crawl into bed to try to forget about today, there is a thump at my window. I open the blinds to look out. There sits Wild Thing, perched on the windowsill. I open the window, and he springs into my arms. As Wild Thing drapes his body over my arms, he purrs so deeply my arms tingle.

"You knew that I needed some extra attention tonight, didn't ya? You can stay for a little while, but we can't let Mother know you're in the house. You know that Mother doesn't allow animals in the house. No roarin', or we'll both get into trouble."

Wild Thing settles at the foot of my bed and falls into a deep sleep.

Forgive and Forget

"I heard those boys talking in the hall about yesterday afternoon. I told Stan if he ever did anything like that again, he would answer to me," Ella declares to our lunch group. Ella is always the first one to stand up for her friends. Besides, Ella is already five feet nine inches tall. Her height can be quite intimidating. She jokes that with her tall genes, she is going to be the next Statue of Liberty. Ella's twin, Grace, says it's OK with her that Ella is taller.

Ella's support is appreciated, but I am even more humiliated because by now, the whole school probably knows about yesterday. It's apparent that sometime, I will have to deal with those boys myself.

The sixth-grade teachers allow us to eat with anyone we want. On the first day of school, the teachers told us we were an orderly group of children and they were certain we could be trusted to use good manners and enjoy some time on our own, so the teachers retire to the lounge to eat in peace and quiet.

Kaylee, Elizabeth, Faith, Lila, Grace, Ella, and I all see the boys smirking and pointing at our table. Ella gives them the evil eye. The boys continue to point and laugh. And then it happens. Like lightning, Ella strikes! She crosses the cafeteria to grab and twist Stan's ear until he winces and whimpers something to Ella. I'm just too embarrassed to let my friend stand up for me, so I force myself to approach the boys' table as well.

I say to Stan, "I don't need for my friend to talk for me. I do want you to know that I think what you did to me yesterday was not nice. Not nice at all! What have I done to you, anyway? I'm not asking for an apology, but is it too much to ask that you treat me with the same respect I treat you?"

Not waiting for an answer, I hurry out of the cafeteria. Hiding behind a stall door in the girl's restroom, I can't wipe away the tears fast enough.

Ella knocks on the door. She asks, "Are you OK? For what it's worth, I think you handled that problem pretty well. Did you know that Stan snapped Grace's bra, too? She's been afraid to tell our mother. I wonder who else he has done that to. Don't worry—you don't have to go back to the cafeteria. Grace took care of your tray."

The rest of my friends meet me at the restroom and surround me like mother hens as we make our way back to the classroom.

The history lesson begins, and when I get up the courage, I look over at Stan. His face turns red as a beet as he looks down at his feet. When he looks up, I smile my forgiveness. Stan smiles back.

Poppy taught me to never hold a grudge. He told me that holding a grudge does more harm to you than to the other person. His motto is "forgive and forget." I hope Stan has been taught the same.

More Than a Math Lesson

Another week of school is gone. Every night, Poppy and I experiment with the tangrams. The class is working on harder equations now. I tell Poppy that Mrs. Buchanan asked me and Ella to help Stan, Graham, and Elizabeth. They just don't understand how to write equations. Mrs. Buchanan gave us some construction paper for cutting out tangram pieces. I thought that it would help if the pieces could first be placed on top of each other to show their relationships. Two medium-sized triangles fit on top of a large triangle. Two small triangles fit on top of a medium-sized triangle. Two small triangles fit on top of a parallelogram, and two small triangles fit on top of the square. We write easy equations like this:

If 1 large triangle = 20 . . . then, 1 medium triangle = 10 . . .
and 1 small triangle = 5
One large triangle = two medium triangles
20 = 10 + 10 or (2 x 10)
20 = 20
3 small triangles + 1 medium triangle - 1 small triangle =
1 medium triangle + 2 small triangles
(3 x 5) + (1 x 10) - (1 x 5) = (1 x 10) + (2 x 5)
(15 + 10) – 5 = 10 + 10
25 - 5 = 20
20 = 20

On Saturday night, I ask Poppy if he wants to write some more equations for Mrs. Buchanan. She really likes our problems.

Poppy surprises me. "Little Chank, I think I've figured out a way to help Stan. His father is helpin' me build that new house over on Longs Fork. Him and I was talkin' about how much Stan likes to build things out of scrap wood. I got this idea that if Stan could feel the actual weight of a tangram and think of a large triangle as bein' the same weight of two medium triangles on a real balance scale, then, he just might understand this concept of equations a lot better."

"Poppy, what a great idea! But I don't have any pieces like that," I say, wishing so much for those pieces.

"Well, it just so happens I've been in the workhouse, tinkerin' with this idea. I had to build a balance scale first. I used your paper tangram pieces for a pattern, and I had to work with allowances for my saw cuts until I got a large triangle to weigh the same as two medium triangles. Took me a while to balance out all seven pieces, but I believe it'll work now. The balance might be slightly off. Want to try it?"

I can't believe my eyes. Poppy cut and lightly sanded the pieces to perfection. When we try them, I just know that Stan will come to understand equations, equalities, and inequalities like a math whiz!

"Poppy, I don't want to sound ungrateful, but I really need two sets of tangram blocks so Stan can do harder problems."

"Well, I'll tell you what. I'll ask Stan's dad to come help me make you several sets. But you try this set out first and see if it fits the need."

At math time on Monday morning, I ask Mrs. Buchanan if Stan, Graham, Elizabeth, Ella, and I have permission to go work in the hall. I explain to Mrs. Buchanan the contents of the box I brought to school, and Mrs. Buchanan finally relents saying, "A try couldn't hurt!"

As we work first easy, then harder problems, Stan catches on. Elizabeth says she likes boys' toys almost as much as she likes her roller skates. She catches on to equations, and there is no stopping her! Graham just wants to play with the balance scale. I figure that's OK since he may figure out something about the relationships of the tangram pieces just from their weights. He does. Poppy knows boys!

Mrs. Buchanan comes to the door and whispers, "Are you children ready for science class?"

Stan answers for us, "Mrs. Buchanan, everybody in class should play with these blocks. I understand those darned equations now. We're writin' some problems for the class."

Mrs. Buchanan replies, "Stan, I believe that Ella and Mary Ann have written more problems than we could ever do in a year's time. But maybe you could write some for your buddies to do after school. I hear you are spending way too much time riding your bikes all over town and bothering folks. Now, come on in for science class. And Mary Ann, could you stay a few minutes after school?"

Stan glances at me and quickly looks away. I hope he doesn't think I've been tattling.

I look at Mrs. Buchanan, wondering if she knows what happened the other day on the sidewalk. She doesn't pay me any particular attention as she hurries back into the classroom to teach about potential and kinetic energy.

I just wonder if my class could make some wind-up toys. Poppy might have some ideas tonight. I can't help but dread that tomorrow will bring more challenges than just learning all about potential and kinetic energy.

One might describe Stan as a body in motion that stays in motion. He is always busy and always full of surprises. In the cafeteria, Stan and his buddies come over to the girls' table, and Stan announces to everyone, "If you haven't used Mary Ann's balance scale and blocks yet, you should give them a try. They're better than any math textbook."

Ella says, "Does this mean you're going to be nice to Mary Ann, Grace, and all us other girls?"

Stan's cheeks turn cherry red. "Yeah. Guess I've been a jerk. Sorry, Mary Ann. Sorry, Grace. Sorry to you, too, Kaylee."

Grace tells Stan he's forgiven, and I tell him I appreciate his apology and that, for what it's worth, I didn't tattle to Mrs. Buchanan. Kaylee just looks down at her tray.

Jay says to Stan, "I told you they would be nice about it."

Graham says, "I believe you have some work cut out for you, though. One ain't too sure about forgivin' you. Are you, Kaylee?"

Kaylee smiles her appreciation at Graham, then looks back down at her tray.

After school, Mrs. Buchanan asks me to show her how the balance scale and tangram blocks work. She says that during recess today, she quizzed Stan on some equations and he was breezing through the problems. Mrs. Buchanan wants me and Ella to present even more difficult problems to our little group.

Thinking about how much fun the tangrams are, I am befuddled when Mrs. Buchanan says, "I want to walk over to your mother's classroom with you after school. I have a question for her."

I'm afraid that the bra incident is going to come up now that the whole thing is resolved—mostly. Ella said she'd work on Kaylee.

Instead of talking about the bra incident, Mrs. Buchanan asks Mother if she thinks Poppy would have time to make a class set of tangram blocks and balance scales. There would be two sets of tangrams and one balance scale for every two students. Mother doubts that Poppy will have that much time, but she promises Mrs. Buchanan that she will ask.

After my teacher leaves, Mother says, "Ella's mother told me what was going on with Stan and his buddies. I'm proud of you and Ella for figuring out a way to resolve the problem on your own. But if there are other problems in the future that you don't feel you can handle, please let me know. Some problems don't resolve themselves so easily. I'm proud that you stood up for yourself. It sounds like Stan feels ashamed for what he did. Maybe he learned a lesson about respecting others. You have been very kind to teach him math in spite of what he did."

"Mother," I ask, "do you and Ella's mom talk about everything that happens in school? There just might be times I don't want you to know everything."

"We only have time to discuss the most important things. I'm afraid Thurston is giving Ella's mom a hard time right now. It seems he wants to sit at the back of the room and read his novels instead of attending to his English lessons. Glad your problems are resolved for the moment. Let's get home and do our chores. The boys will be coming home late tonight. They have to go over to Coeburn for a scrimmage. We'll have to pick up the slack."

As a whole, today turned out just fine. I'm thinking that Grandfather Tang, like me, had more than just a math problem to solve. For now, though, it seems that things are going to be just fine at my new school in town.

Christmastime Already?!

"Poppy, I believe you and I have created a monster. Stan is a math nut now! Stan, Ella, Elizabeth, Graham, and I taught the whole class how to use the tangrams. Mrs. Buchanan even lets us go to the other classes to teach. Just one problem, though: Mrs. Buchanan is so protective of the balance scales and tangram blocks that she preaches to every class about takin' care of them. Poppy, I do mean preach! She even threatens that if a bag holdin' the tangram blocks gets torn up, it will have to be repaired or replaced. Mrs. Buchanan says that Mommy Laurie and Ella's grandmother Eleanor worked too hard to make the bags in the first place. I agree, but it's a little embarrassing!

"It did take you and Stan's and Ella's dads a long time to make all those tangram pieces. Stan brags about you all the time to the other kids. He liked helpin', you know. He told the boys about all the neat tools you have in your workshop. Have you and Mommy read all the thank-you notes yet?" I ask.

"Yes. I believe you go to school with some mighty nice children, Little Chank. I feel a lot better now about ya goin' to school in town. One of your classmates, his name is Eddie, asked me if I had a job for his dad. The steel mill where Eddie's dad was workin' installed some automated machines. There was a cutback, and Eddie's dad lost his job. His dad brought the family all the way from Pittsburg thinkin' he had a minin' job waitin' for him. When he got here, the position was filled. Eddie says that his dad did repairs on rental properties for some extra cash. If his dad has some good carpentry skills, I shore could use him. Would you take this note to Eddie for him to give his dad?"

Not surprised at how concerned Poppy gets over other people's problems, I put the note in my math book to take to school.

The weeks fly by so quickly that it is already time for Christmas! Eddie's dad is helping Poppy and Stan's dad finish the inside of the new home on Longs Fork. Stan tells me that his dad really likes working for my grandfather. Stan's dad says that Poppy treats all the workers with respect and pays fair wages. I'm not a bit surprised.

With Saturday chores done, Mommy, Aunt Tess, and Mother discuss the upcoming Christmas festivities. Lizzie and I go shuck and shell corn. She isn't talking so babyish anymore. It's fun to watch her grow.

The farm is running pretty smoothly. Most of the heifers and dams will calve come spring, so we shouldn't have the problems of last winter.

It's grooming day for Lassie. Lizzie and I head back to the farmhouse. We put Lassie on the grooming table in the utility room. Wild Thing decides he wants to be groomed, too. He floats up to the table and lies beside Lassie.

I ask Lizzie, "Do you want to groom Wild Thing? This is the first time he's jumped on the table. He's never been groomed before. It's goin' to take me a while to get these mats out of Lassie's fur. Don't know how she got in such a mess!"

"Blackie likes to get groomed. Did you know that I've been bwushin' Wild Thing, too? He loves it!" Lizzie proudly tells me.

"I didn't know you had been groomin' the cats. No wonder Wild Thing jumped up on the table. Wild Thing must have forgiven you for yanking his tail. Lizzie, you are saying your r's and l's better. You are learning a lot in first grade. I'm so proud of you."

"Thanks. I trwy real hard in school. The other kids make fun of me sometimes, but Miss Kelly says I'm learnin' fast. I like her a lot."

"Well, you just keep workin' hard. Christmas is comin', you know. What is Santa goin' to bring you?" I ask. I already know that I will be getting new shoes. My black-and-white oxfords are so tight, my toes hurt. We are going to Bristol over the holidays to shop for clothes for all of us. Mother says it's just too hard to figure sizes for four fast-growing children when ordering clothes from Montgomery Ward. We'll have to try on the clothes to make sure they fit and still allow room to grow.

Early in the fall, we had a family conference. Mother went over household and clothing expenses and the request from Stuart at D & S Supermarket for more fresh vegetables this coming summer. Mother no longer has enough money to give us an allowance, so on Saturdays, Dale services cars at the gas station down on Rock House Road and Kyle services cars for the big dealership in town. Thurston makes money from the sale of his eggs, but most of that goes into his college fund. And I don't earn any money at all. I don't know what my brothers and I will get Mother, Mommy, and Poppy for Christmas this year.

Lizzie brings me back to what I asked her. "I want some more clothes for my Chatty Cathy doll. And I want a coloring book and a new box of crwayons. What do you want?"

"Well, I want...I want to...never mind. I'm going to have to think about it."

"Aunt 'Tine, Mary Ann doesn't know what she wants for Christmas. What do you want?" Lizzie asks Mother as she comes to get a jar of kraut out of the pantry in the utility room.

"What I want is for everyone to be happy and healthy, and that should be a gracious plenty for anyone, don't you agree?" Mother asks Lizzie.

"I want everybody to be happy and healthy, too." Lizzie parrots.

At suppertime this first night of Christmas vacation, Mother laments that we neglected some housecleaning this fall. Kyle looks at Dale, Dale looks at Thurston, and Thurston looks at me. We know what our Christmas gift to Mother is going to be!

Next day, Dale calls Miss McCoy and asks her to get Mother away for a day. Miss McCoy invites Mother to go to Roanoke to do Christmas shopping. Mommy Laurie convinces Mother that she needs a day off and time to chat with her good friend.

Mother's day off comes and we start work early. Mommy Laurie, my brothers, and I vacuum, mop, turn mattresses, change the sheets, polish the pine floors, polish the furniture, clean the windows, and dust the baseboards. One by one, the jobs on Mother's list that she keeps posted in the kitchen get checked off.

When we finish, Kyle puts a note on the front door.

Mother,

We are doing our chores. Mommy is holding supper for you. She said for you to come straight to her house when you get home.

Kyle

Mommy keeps Mother talking about her trip until Kyle and Dale return from milking and Thurston and I bring in the eggs. Mommy says, "Well, we shore have worked hard today. I had the children to do some extra chores for me. It's goin' to be bedtime soon. I heard the children say that you had a lot of housecleanin' to catch up on tomorrow. You'll need to git up early, from the sound of that to-do list you made out. In fact, all of us need to git to bed early."

That's our cue to walk Mother home. When we get to the house, Kyle opens the door and turns on the living room light. Mother steps into a room that sparkles and smells like lemon oil.

Mother's jaw drops. She is speechless but manages to ask, "Who in the world did all this work?"

Kyle says, "Come see the rest of the house."

As Mother walks through the house, she keeps repeating to herself, "I don't believe it! I don't believe it! Who did all this work?"

Dale answers, "We all did, Mother. Mommy helped, too. This is our Christmas present to you. Merry Christmas, Mother!"

One would think that we were handing Mother the moon.

Mother sits down on the sofa and looks at each one of us, saying, "How could I be so fortunate to have four such wonderful children? Just one little thing, though," Mother continues with a sheepish grin. "You don't think you could finish the ironing, do you?" Mother chuckles and begins to dab her eyes with the tissue that Thurston hands her.

Thurston mimics the cultured voice of an English butler. "Well, madam, as a matter of fact, the laundry service will deliver tomorrow. Your cousin Emma was glad to have some extra cash for Christmas and offered to do the job for a fee that Mommy and Poppy helped pay. Now, what other jobs might you have for us?"

Mother laughs and declares, "I believe my wishes have been met, sir. You are all most capable servants. Thank you from the bottom of my heart. By the way, Mary Ann, you're going to get that ride in the Piper Cub. Boys, you get a ride, too. Mark is going to fly you over the gorge at Breaks Interstate Park and over the top of Birch Knob. He knows the mountains will 'stun you with their beauty'—his words, not mine! He'll let us know what days will be good for him. It will take four trips because the Piper Cub only holds one passenger at a time, so be patient for your turn. Merry Christmas, children."

It just doesn't matter to me anymore whether or not there are gifts under the Christmas tree, because I get gifts every day. Gifts are everywhere! Gifts like . . .

- a new school I like as much as my old one
- a new haircut—Mother doesn't have time to braid my hair every morning when a shorter ponytail is easy enough for me to fix.
- an extra fried apple pie or chicken biscuit in my lunch box for a classmate who may be hungry
- a grandmother willing to tell a little white lie for something good
- a grandfather who talks to me like I'm a grown-up
- brothers who look out for me
- kind aunts and uncles and cousins and friends
- fireworks on the mountaintop in late summer
- a cat that likes me as much as I like him
- a mother who understands a girl's problems
- grandparents who show their love more than they speak it

I now realize there are gifts too numerous to be counted. At last, I know why every Christmas Day, my grandfather repeats his words from the year before: "Now, children, always remember this: We don't need gifts under the tree, because the best gift of all is the gift of each other."

As I try to go to sleep, I wonder about how my todays will become my tomorrows. I wonder how many more stories our mountain will tell, how many more lessons our mountain will teach, and how many more secrets our mountain will keep. There is one secret I want the mountain to keep; I hope Mother never learns that Wild Thing sleeps at the foot of my bed every night!

Author's Notes

I have heard the story of the Christmas cat since childhood. This version has my own take of the legend, but the reader can research this legend and its many origins.

Many versions of the Grandfather Tang tales have been told in the Chinese culture for thousands of years. The version used in this book is fabricated. Ann Tompert uses the tangrams to tell a beautiful tale in her book *Grandfather Tang's Story.*

My little cousin did not get the Chatty Cathy doll until 1960 when it first came on the market. In this book, she supposedly received the doll in 1958. Chatty Cathy and my cousin did indeed have beautiful matching dresses made by my mother.

The epitaph, "They gave their today for our tomorrow," is inscribed on my grandparents' grave marker. The Kohima Epitaph was reworded to fit the sacrifices that my grandparents made for our family. The quote is actually based on the Kohima Epitaph inscribed on the monument unveiled at Kohima in 1944. For more information, go to www.kohimamuseum.co.uk/kohima-epitaph.

A visit to the Salt Park and the Museum of the Middle Appalachians in Saltville, Virginia, offers a glimpse into how the Civil War came to Southwest Virginia.

Find more information about the mountains of Virginia through these websites:

Breaks Interstate Park, www.breakspark.com
Ralph Stanley Museum and Traditional Music Center, www.ralphstanleymuseum.com
Virginia's Heritage Music Trail, www.thecrookedroad.org
Dickenson County Coal Miners Memorial, www.dickenson411.com/memorial.html

Guided reading activities and extended math activities using tangrams can be downloaded for free on my website.

CPSIA information can be obtained
at www.ICGtesting.com
Printed in the USA
FFOW01n1935151214
9568FF